MW01624127

INCI

BOOKS IN THE STELLAR GUILD SERIES

Tau Ceti by Kevin J. Anderson & Steven Savile

Reboots by Mercedes Lackey & Cody Martin

On The Train by Harry Turtledove & Rachel Turtledove

When the Blue Shift Comes by Robert Silverberg & Alvaro Zinos-Amaro

New Under the Sun by Nancy Kress & Therese Pieczynski

The Aethers of Mars by Eric Flint and Charles E. Gannon

Red Tide by Larry Niven, Brad R. Torgersen and Matthew J. Harrington

Wishing on a Star by Jody Lynn Nye and Angelina Adams

INCI

MIKE RESNICK

WITH

TINA GOWER

THE STELLAR GUILD SERIES

TEAM-UPS WITH BESTSELLING AUTHORS

MIKE RESNICK

SERIES EDITOR

an imprint of

Rockville, Maryland

Series edited by Mike Resnick.

ISBN: 978-1-61242-266-4

Published by Phoenix Pick
an imprint of Arc Manor
P. O. Box 10339
Rockville, MD 20849-0339
www.ArcManor.com

To
Shahid Mahmud:
friend, publisher, and the power
behind ***Stellar Guild*** books

☼

CONTENTS

Introduction to INCI

Greetings, and welcome to another Stellar Guild book. The first few in the series have sold well enough that we can safely predict that the Stellar Guild will be around for a while, and that can only bode well for the future of science fiction because the purpose of the Stellar Guild is to team a top science fiction writer up with a protégé of his/her own choosing. The established pro writes a novella, the protégé writes a novella or a long novelette, a sequel or prequel set in the same universe, and shares a book that's guaranteed to get him or her better exposure than 98% of first novels do.

Our first seven Stellar Guild books featured Kevin J. Anderson, Mercedes Lackey, Harry Turtledove, Robert Silverberg, Nancy Kress, Eric Flint, and Larry Niven and their proteges. For this, the eighth book in the series, it was my turn to write with a protégé, and I think you'll agree that I made a wise choice when I selected Tina Gower. Tina, a former psychologist, is the winner of the $5,000 Golden Pen Award from Writers of the Future, as well as the Daphne du Maurier Prize in the Paranormal Romantic Mystery category and the Romance Writers of America Golden Heart Award. In addition, she has sold four stories to Galaxy's Edge magazine – and it was she, not I, who first noted the slight spelling deviation that forms the basis of this book.

—*Mike Resnick*

INCI

Book One

The Barker Testament

TINA GOWER

The church didn't send the missionary call to everyone. I scanned the list briefly, noting a few similarities amongst the invited. First, each person called had served no less than fifteen years. All the names I recognized were more than forty years old, and all were widowed or unmarried. I gathered the New Worlds Protestant Association was searching for ministers that were dedicated, unattached, and expendable.

And I, Rev. Joshua Barker, was on the list.

I shouldn't have been surprised at the call. The past year I had been encouraged by Bishop Cain to expand my horizons. I'd signed up for every committee, every special interest group. Extra hand in the soup kitchen? I volunteered. An extra service on Sunday? I arranged and performed it. The Bishop subsequently raised concerns of spreading myself too thin.

Semi-retirement was mentioned, and gardening. As I stared with glassy eyes at the sickly huddle of overwatered plants on the front porch, I realized maybe I had dived into my work with too much enthusiasm. Amelia was the gardener.

But why me? Why did I have to go? Not only had God deemed me unworthy of children, a wife who would live into old age with me, success in my profession, he was now casting me out of Earth? He was taking me away from the planet where he had sent his only son to die for our sins?

Adam and Eve had it easy.

Filled with doubt, I turned to an authority on the matter.

I pulled my worn Bible from the shelf and squeezed my eyes shut. I opened to a random page, pointed. I peeked at the selection and sighed. Joshua 1:9. Of course it would be my namesake.

Have not I commanded thee? Be strong and of a good courage; be not afraid, neither be thou dismayed: for the Lord thy God is with thee whithersoever thou goest.

Well, I suppose that is as clear an answer as any.

Drafting my letter of farewell to my congregation took the rest of my day and well into the night. It was hard to sum up the gratitude and experiences of more than twenty years in a few paragraphs. In the end, it read like sorrow-filled poetry chiseled on an epitaph.

If God had truly called me to this task, then who am I to leave it unanswered?

⁂

Who am I? A fool. The only explanation of my character was to believe God had sent me to some great duty.

A group of us stepped off of the transport ship into the stifling humidity of Kaus, where I'd spend the next ten years on my missionary expedition. Still groggy and foggy from rotated shifts of cryosleep, the crew and passengers huddled into loose bevies categorized by association. I stood off to the side, clearly on my own.

The dim light of a distant star glowed on the horizon. A crewmember passed out safety glasses that provided better vision in the darkness of the planet. Tendrils of steam swirled from the cracks in the rocks, dancing in the air like lazy ghosts.

Captain Williams climbed onto a large rock with little effort—not that she needed a stage; the woman's personality and charisma created an illusion that she was taller and broader than anyone else on the ship by at least a foot in either direction. I slipped on my safety glasses and watched orange steam-like dust swirl around her. "We'll have tents set up in the next hour. We're going to work to get the temporary housing units up before the end of the week. And permanent units will be completed in six months."

Dr. Ira Beckerman shuffled off the transport ship carrying a box of first aid supplies. "Christ, it's hot as Hell down here."

Several of the other researchers around us laughed nervously and glanced at me. I smiled and nodded to Ira.

"Oh, sorry, Reverend."

"Welcome to your new home," the captain's voice rang out, echoing off the walls of the canyon where we'd set up camp.

"Okay, museum crew over here!" A woman waved her arms enthusiastically. A quarter of the crowd filed her direction.

"McCade Research, team one!" yelled another man.

Shouts echoed in every direction, bringing order to the chaos of arrival, until I was standing alone.

I clutched my worn Bible flipping through the pages. The faint scent of vanilla filtered through my breathing apparatus, reminding me of home. I swallowed what felt like a wad of rubber in my throat.

The teams gathered equipment, leaving it in piles. Some left to get started on research, as if the ten year minimum commitment wouldn't be enough time to gather it all.

I leaned against the wall of rock wondering where to begin. I closed my eyes and pointed my finger on a random page. Opened and read. I'd landed on a random page in Genesis, and I glared at the long list of who begat whom. Not exactly helpful, but then again there weren't many scriptures that would explain how to convert an alien race to Christianity.

Ira walked by with a group of other anthropologists and waved. "I'll see you at the game table tonight after the safety meeting? Maybe some cards this time?"

I forced a smile. "Sure."

When the crew cleared out, I hefted my bag onto a flat rock—as good an altar as any, and stared at the planet Captain Williams had declared my new home. Dark, hot—I tried not to draw the obvious underworld conclusion that Ira had.

Not that any place without Amelia would ever be a real home.

I moved my personal items away from the steam, so my candles wouldn't melt. Scientists had predicted the planet would have a generally cold weather pattern, but didn't account for the extensive geothermal activity under the surface. This area in particular had higher activity, and was aptly named the "The Steam Fields." The planet was roughly twice the size of Earth, more gravity, which made me feel heavier, like I'd walked through mud, and the constant steam was as if I'd never left my shower.

The life on Kaus wasn't advanced, but Kausians possessed the ability to reply to short simple messages to human scouting ships. We'd deemed the Kausians as non-hostile and our language program could translate simple messages between our people.

I continued to unpack items from my bag, checking and rechecking my water ration. I fumbled with the oxygen tubes that wrapped around my face and secured it behind my neck. There was breathable air on the planet, but the higher carbon dioxide levels, which trapped warmer air in the atmosphere, wouldn't be healthy to breathe for long periods of time.

A group of Kausians clustered and crouched watching me from a few feet away. Raised to full height, the Kausians were as tall as my waist. Some only reached my knees.

"I'm here to tell you a bit about our beliefs on Earth." I held up my tattered Bible. "This is just one of many. I hope you find the stories enjoyable. And I'd love to talk about your customs, too."

A number the Kausians moved closer. Aware of my audience, I flipped open to a random page and read a hymn. Then did my own version of Bible roulette to find a story and clicked the translator on, so my new friends would enjoy the tale.

Not that it mattered, the translation software was crude and I doubted they'd find interest in a religion on another planet they never knew existed until recently. I could have started on Adam and Eve, heck I could read from a recipe book, but the Bible opened to Moses parting the Red Sea.

As I read the group inched closer and I was able to make out their forms. We'd been sent images from other expedition groups, but in person the aliens looked even more peculiar.

Their bodies were separated into three segments, the top part being the head where two filmy white ovals protruded from the sides and an opening at the bottom of the head where a tongue-like appendage would snake out every few seconds and "taste" the air. Their bodies consisted of a dark iridescent exoskeleton, short legs, and two sets of long arms. At the end of the lower set of arms were pincher claws, and the top set had four pronged digits that they used as hands.

"The steam!" they cried when I got the part where the sea collapses on the Egyptian soldiers. "He is of the steam!"

I had no idea what 'the steam' meant to them, but I was encouraged that they were excited.

When the story was done, I closed the Bible. The group stared back at me. I didn't know how to relate to these creatures, so I continued on with my sermon, describing the story in plain simple terms and then asked, "What did Moses see on the mountain?"

The creatures wobbled in place.

"What did God tell Moses to do?"

Still nothing. Two of the creatures turned and walked away.

Maybe something more basic? After all they'd eventually need to understand the meaning of God. "Explain in your own words what you think God is?"

They clicked their claws together and their tongues flicked in rapid succession, but none of them answered.

"Who do you believe created your planet?"

They slowly wandered around, checking my supplies, but not touching anything, and then left. I'd never taught Sunday school; maybe if I had I'd have been more skilled at keeping their interest. Amelia was the teacher. She'd have had them riveted by her every word.

Complete indifference by the native population: at least the report of initial contact I'd send to the New Worlds Church would be brief. They should have sent someone who had experience with introducing religion to people who'd never heard of it.

I sat on the altar, found a good book on my tablet, and read for the rest of the afternoon. The strain of packing and unpacking caught up to me and my eyelids drooped closed. I could probably stand ten years of this. Maybe this was God's way of forced retirement.

"Excuse me, Father?" A young woman tapped my shoulder. She gave a half-smile and hooked an unruly brown lock of hair behind her ear. "Father Barker?"

I blinked awake, rubbing my face. "It's Reverend," I said. "Father is generally a Catholic term for priests."

Her eyes lowered and she held her bottom lip between her teeth. "Oh, I'm so sorry. I don't know much about spiritual matters..." She brought her gaze to mine, although it seemed with some effort. "...which is why I was hoping to discuss a few scriptures."

Now this was a surprise. I'd been unaware of other believers on the voyage to Kaus. Early in the journey, between cryosleep cycles, I'd started a spiritual group only to have few attendees. And those who did come were more interested in a debate on why I assumed aliens needed to be 'saved' and quite frankly I agreed, but not for the same reasons—God gave us his only son—on Earth. Nowhere in the Bible did it provide a roadmap to save anyone else.

She held out her hand. "Lena Sanchez. I'm one of the cultural anthropologists for the Museum Project. We're collecting alien artifacts for study and display."

"I'm on my way to meet a friend for the safety meeting," I said. "He's actually with the Museum Project, too. Perhaps you could join us for tea and a game after the meeting while we discuss the scriptures?"

She checked her schedule. "I've got a meeting directly after the safety meeting, but it's near the rec tent, maybe I can join you later? We can walk to the safety meeting together."

On our 'walk' which was more of a jog, I learned Lena didn't do anything slow. She talked quickly and efficiently. "When we jumped into Faster Than Light travel our time stays the same and years go by in real time for every minute we travel.

People we know—knew, they're long gone." She cleared her throat. "It hasn't quite hit me yet."

"I'm familiar with the phenomenon." Even though I barely understood it. We stopped and I placed my hand on a boulder to catch my breath.

"One of my jobs is to scan the data coming in from other museum teams stationed on the neighboring planets. It's all coming in so fast. Years and years of data on other recovery missions collected while we were in FTL. One of those planets is Astik. Are you familiar with Astik?"

"No."

"Researchers discovered evidence of an extinct alien culture and millions of cliff and cave drawings. Fa—Reverend, we've worked out several translations of the drawings and you'll never guess what they found. Let's set up a meeting some time and I'll discuss the findings. Many people believe it could point to proof in the existence of God."

Of course. I've been banished to a distant planet to preach the word of God to a group of aliens who may never believe. Meanwhile, Christianity was making a comeback on Earth. "I don't know how I can help. It sounds like everything is in order."

"It is, except," a blush crept up her neck and into her cheeks. "When I was young my parents explained to me how religion is scientifically impossible, and now..."

"You're curious."

She nodded. "Yes."

So God had sent me on a mission to convert a planet of aliens and one human. "You're welcome to attend any of the services here and if work keeps you busy I'm in the rec area most evenings."

"Thank you. I'll stop by tonight after my meeting."

I heard a click and scrape sound. Lena paused, tilting her head. We both spoke at the same time.

"—Did you hear that?"

"—What was that sound?"

As the clicking continued, Lena searched the section of the cliff. It looked as though the mountain had given away hundreds of years ago, leaving large grooves and crevices. White vine plants crisscrossed the surface of the mound.

Lena knelt behind the boulders and turned on her translator. "Hello there."

I peered over her shoulder. A Kausian hid in the crack of two boulders that towered over us. His tongue skimmed Lena's hands and he flinched away.

"I'm sorry, my mistake." Lena stepped back. "I'm too close."

He looked at me, or at least I think he looked at me. It was hard to tell, their eyes were like large inset golf balls and as far as I could see, no pupils to focus.

"The man who can move the dust. He is of the steam," the Kausian said to me, but Lena's translator decoded the message.

I turned my translator on. "What was that?"

His claws tapped against the rock. "He moved the dust."

"Were you at the sermon?" I asked. "Do you mean Moses?"

"He is of the steam," he said again.

"Moses parted the Red Sea. It's a place on our planet." I slowly pulled my tablet from my backpack. "Would you like to see a picture?"

"No," he said. "I would like to see him part the dust."

"I don't have any video of that, it happened before we had recording devices. Also, he parted water." I tipped my water canteen, letting the wetness flow between my fingers. "Water. Liquid."

"Yes," he said.

"Would you like to touch it?" Lena grabbed her own canteen and moved toward him, but whatever interest held him there broke and he scampered up the side of the cliff.

"Wow. Fast little climber," I said.

"Darn it!" Lena thrust her canteen into her holster. "We've had no luck communicating with them all day." She eyed me. "He seemed very intent on you though."

I held up my hands. "Don't look at me. I had no luck communicating at the sermon. This," I gestured to the mound, "this was an anomaly."

She gave me a look that told me she didn't believe me. "Hm, well, we'd better get going so we don't miss the meeting."

She walked ahead, but I was pulled to the direction the alien went. I scanned the path he'd taken, no sign of him.

"Are you coming?" Lena called.

I caught a glint of white in my glasses at the top of the rocks. "Lena," I whispered. The glint moved along the ridge and for a moment I thought our friend would return. Curious to speak to him, I didn't think anyone at the sermon had grasped the story. But this little guy did—I wanted to talk with him.

When Lena didn't respond I glanced at her, she looked at me, her head tilted to the side.

"Reverend?"

I pointed at the top of the ridge at...nothing. I blew out a breath, the one I didn't know I was holding. "Never mind." I massaged my forehead, a tension headache already forming.

We arrived at the safety meeting and I walked around looking for Ira, who was nowhere in sight. We got a long-winded talk from one of the engineers on the geothermal activity of the planet, what areas were safe, how to use our suits. When the meeting was adjourned, people rushed off in various directions, indicating they found the material as boring as I did.

I headed to the rec tent to meet Ira. He sat in the lounge, hunched over a lenticular table behind a thick fabric curtain. Ira swiped through the air at the projected deck of cards and they shuffled while he leaned into the beige chair cushions and sipped his tea. His look of bliss evaporated and morphed into chagrin when he noticed me.

"Don't give me that gloomy look," he said. "This would be the only way I could get a decent seat here. If I waited with you at that damn meeting, we'd be stuck with a crappy table."

I pointedly glanced around the empty area of the tent, scooted a chair from a nearby table, and sighed. "Ira, you had the idea to go to the meeting first. We could have skipped this one."

"But this way I reserved the best seats in the rec tent at the best time of day." His mouth quirked into a half-grin, which would have given him the expression of a toddler sneaking candy were it not for his hooknose, bushy eyebrows, and salt and pepper hair.

"I met a colleague of yours. Dr. Sanchez." I grabbed the makings for Chamomile tea.

Ira snorted. "And survived to tell the tale. I'm surprised Sanchez took a break from work to go."

I wagged my finger. "She was nice. And besides, at least she showed. You're not going to have a clue what to do when your suit overheats. None of us will want to take the time to tell you."

He shrugged and studied the new cards spread in the air above the table. "I'll go to the next one."

I scratched my neck. "Dr. Sanchez had some information on an extinct race that might prove the existence of God."

His finger paused mid-flick; the King of Spades suspended in the air. "Interesting." He slouched in the chair, eyes narrowed, but a grin twitching on his lips. "Are you telling me as a polite suggestion to consider the good word?"

I smiled at his joke. "I'm just making conversation."

"Bull, nobody just mentions Jesus to a Jewish guy as an ice-breaker." He shook his head and sipped his drink.

"I didn't mention Jesus."

"He was coming next. It's like egg and toast, peanut butter and jelly, chocolate and wine. Whenever a Christian mentions God, Jesus follows right behind."

"You know I completely regret ever agreeing to go on this mission."

"It's been nice getting to know you too."

"But, there is this small part of me that still thinks things happen for a reason. Dr. Sanchez really believes that this discovery points to answers to the question of spirituality. Tease me all you want, just don't ruin it for her."

"You think I'll be the one to spoil that? There are thousands of documented religions across the universe, and Christians still justify ways to think they've found the right one." He snorted and continued his game.

"I don't think the inhabitants of Kaus will care much about religions on other planets, but some humans might want to rediscover their spirituality based on the news." Perhaps it was my true purpose being stationed here.

"I'll play nice. Don't worry. If there's trouble it won't come from me." He said it like he expected trouble regardless.

Captain Williams pulled up a seat next to us. "We gonna start this game or is the Reverend going to bore us with a sermon?"

I swiped the deck and flipped though the game selection. "I don't preach to atheists."

"Oh come on. You're practically an atheist yourself, just haven't admitted it." Williams ordered a black coffee, as she settled into her chair. "Why exactly did you agree to come? Ten years of your life on a mission on Kaus, is a heck of a sacrifice for God."

I'd sacrificed more than that, but I wasn't going to give her the satisfaction of admitting my doubts out loud.

Dr. Sanchez poked her head around the curtain. "Dr. Beckermann?" Then her gaze swept toward Williams and me. Her deep brown lashes fluttered. She raked a shaky hand through her bun, where more hair spilled out than managed to stay in the pins. "Oh, I'm sorry. I didn't mean to interrupt."

"Dr. Sanchez," Ira said, his tone more a warning than a greeting.

"Sit right down, Dear," I said and Ira shot me a death glare.

"Lena if this is about work, it's after work hours. I don't work after hours," Ira said.

I laughed. "You don't work during work hours either."

She inched into the room. "Well, it's not exactly work."

"Then why did you call me Dr. Beckermann and not Ira? You call me Dr. Beckermann—I assume it's for work."

"Dr. Beckermann—"

He threw his hands over his head. "See, there you go again."

"Deal her in," said Williams.

Lena ignored both of them. "I would love to discuss the Astik artifacts. Particularly the cliff drawings and their mentions of a savior type figure in their history."

"I've been reading those reports as well." Capt. Williams stepped between us. "It's just another primitive religion that developed on a distant planet. My understanding is the translations are rough at best."

"But it doesn't appear the translations are too far off." Lena frowned and placed her hand on the lenticular table to grant access.

Ira sighed and kicked his feet up onto the table, as if he were resigned to Lena's impromptu work session.

She flicked through several pictures before pausing on one. She expanded the picture on the display, drawing her hands up and out, and the carving filled our corner of the room. The sharp speckled granite lined the walls and formed a labyrinth. The smooth surface was covered with pocked chips, smooth groves from water, and chiseled symbols. She changed the settings and translations overlapped the glyphs.

She moved the carvings in front of us. "Reverend Barker, there are a few symbols that seem to tell a story of a savior of some type. What is your knowledge of other religions?"

"I know Christianity best, but in seminary school we were required to read other religious texts and participate in an exchange program with other religions. I don't mind offering my services if you have any questions."

The captain interrupted. "You'll still get a Christian bias. And who wrote the language software that's performing the translations? Humans. And humans are drawing the conclusions to its meaning. Don't you think there could be bias in the translations?"

"It's the best we have to go off of." Lena crossed her arms and pressed her lips together. The Captain and Lena appeared engaged a silent debate involving stiff body language and angry eyes.

"We'll have all of tomorrow to sort this out and scour the universe for more experts. Dr. Sanchez is anything if not thorough," Ira said.

Lena smiled. "Thank you, Dr. Beckermann."

"Okay, work session over. Now you call me Ira." Ira swept the glyphs to the side and brought out the cards. "We can discuss the findings again tomorrow. Let's get this game started."

A few hours and significantly fewer credits later, Dr. Sanchez walked away the victor.

I spent the next few days performing sermons and showing the Kausians various ceremonies. They appeared to have a genuine interest that grew after each meeting, although they never spoke except a few random words here and there. Dr. Sanchez joined several of the meetings, which was a relief to have at least one participant asking questions and engaging in discussion. A few times Dr. Beckermann joined as well, to attempt to communicate with the Kausians with no success.

As the week progressed, Sanchez and Beckermann switched their efforts to search for artifacts to trade for various museum buyers. I was left again to fend for myself among the Kausians. I unrolled a woven rug over a flat rock surface and set up a number of items. I'd brought a bowl, some water, a towel, and my Bible.

A group of Kausians gathered while I set up, snapping their claws and striking their tongues into the hot air.

I started to pour the water into the bowl and then eyed a crevasse in the rock where liquid bubbled from below the surface. I'd learned the liquid was water, although slightly acidic. It would corrode my bowl, but I figured my audience would appreciate the gesture.

The water steamed from my ceramic and I placed it on the ground. Their tongues darted out in rapid motions simultaneously. My heart beat in the same rhythm—I didn't know what to expect. I explained my intention, pointed to the foot of the alien closest to me.

"In the ceremony I wash the feet of one of the visitors," I said.

Tongues darted in every direction, but none of the aliens attempted to communicate, even though they knew it was possible through the translator.

"Please. I mean no harm. This is to show my deep gratitude for welcoming us to your world." I didn't know how else to explain the significance of the event, and decided to keep it simple.

A number of the spectators on the outskirts hobbled away in the direction of the village, about a half-dozen remained.

"Foot in?" One of the aliens asked. The translator cackled the message attempt. A crewmember had explained it would take a few days for the program to get better at learning the language. Until then we'd mumble through. The more we spoke the faster it could do its job.

"Yes. Just dip your foot in the liquid." I'd seen a number the Kausians walking through the muddy pathways, so I knew the liquid would not harm them. I donned protective gloves. We all wore thin body suits to lower our exposure to alien disease until we were able to stabilize our immune system with various inoculations. "I will wash your feet."

The alien then slammed his lower arm appendage into the bowl. The liquid splashed over the sides. I didn't want to correct it, so I dutifully washed his pincher claw and dried it with a towel. When I finished it sauntered off. Three more spectators followed and after a distance they stopped and inspected the washed claw.

I tapped the bowl to get the attention of the remaining two. "Would you both like me to wash your feet as well?"

They both plopped their claws into the bowel together and pushed each other aside. "My feet. My feet." They both exclaimed.

"No need to argue." If that was indeed what they were doing, it seemed almost as if they were playing the way they daintily shoved each other. "I will wash you both."

They settled and I gently washed them together and wondered if they were a family of some sort, perhaps a mated pair. They appeared familiar with one another. When I was done they both scampered off.

Then I began the second part of the service where I presented the body of Christ, dehydrated bread wafers, and the group inspected them while I read the story of Jesus' last supper. I stopped to explain every few lines. They looked curious—or what I guessed was curiosity. Sometimes I wondered if I was reading too closely into their emotions.

For the rest of the day I wandered the area to see if I could learn their culture, perhaps some of their customs, and this would help me choose my sermon for tomorrow.

The creatures lived in clefts dug out of the rocky surface. What appeared as a hill of rocks and boulders was in fact a home to several Kausians. I meandered along a worn path through the village. Small dots of vegetation crept along the hillside sporadically. According to Captain Williams this was one of the less advanced settlements on the planet.

I wandered for a ways until I noticed a gravel crunching sound of someone following me. I turned and my follower scurried into a fissure.

"I'm sorry!" I called out. "I didn't mean to frighten you."

No answer.

I vowed to be more careful. This species was more bashful than I'd anticipated. Along my stroll many of the Kausians peeked from their homes in the rock; some of the smaller ones would come closer and touch my clothing, flinching when it swayed. I noticed symbols scratched into the surface of the homes: wide-set "Y" overlapping "t" shape, as if someone grabbed hold of the arms of the letter, bent them downward, and added smaller barbs at the bottom.

Again, I noted a follower. I glanced behind me to see if it was the same fellow. He had a marking on his leg, one that seemed different than the others, but to be honest they all looked the same. Once I established myself, I hoped I'd be more observant. I memorized the different color markings on his legs and managed to confirm that he was my shadow through the rock village.

I sat on the ground; my feet ached from the extra gravity. The muscles in my neck and back burned. I massaged the offending areas with my fingers, and sipped from my canteen. My tracker hung back.

"I'd love to talk with you," I said. "I hope to share and exchange information from our cultures and learn from one another."

I didn't know if it was a he or a she or neither. I'd have to remember to ask the researchers at the camp for more general knowledge about their species. If I could get my shadow to open up, maybe I could even ask him. I decided to call the Kausian a "him" for now. I shoved away the guilty feeling for the assumption, but it did make it easier for me. I'd make a point to find out the proper terms.

"Do you have a name? Something to call you by?" I pointed to myself. "My name is Joshua Barker."

"Joshua Barker," he pointed to himself. And just when I was about to correct him, he emitted a series of clicks that the translator didn't pick up on. This must have been his name.

"I didn't catch that. Our translators aren't working as well as we'd like. Can I call you Click?"

"Yes."

"Okay, Click, what do you do? What is your profession? Do you have a job?"

His tongue flicked in the air at each question as if he were trying to decipher my meaning by tasting my words.

"Job. I have one," he said. And then he stepped forward and using his claw he drew the Y symbol in the gravel. "This." He backed away from me.

"I don't understand. Are you an artist?"

His tongue flicked.

I decided to let the question go and offered my own information. "I'm a spiritual leader."

"I do not understand," Click said.

I laughed. "Huh. Well then, I guess we're even." I motioned for him to come closer and he did, hesitantly. I eased my Bible from my knapsack. "This is a special book to me. We keep stories of a great man in here. An important man on our world—I tell his story." It was as simple an explanation as I could think of and the translator should pick up at least some of it.

Click analyzed my book, tapping on the cover a few times with his upper arms. "The man who parts the dust."

I heart raced. Could it be the same Kausian Dr. Sanchez and I encountered our first night here?

He then retracted his appendage and motioned to me, almost mimicking my earlier gesture. "I will show you things."

"Thank you. I'd be honored," I said.

"You will follow me," he said. I was pleased the translator had begun to pick up more of the language.

He hobbled in front of me. Then I noticed he favored his right side, where he had the markings that were different than the others of his kind. Did he have an injury? Was he old or young?

"What is wrong with your leg?" I ventured, my curiosity getting the best of me.

Click paused and then tasted the air. "I walk with it." He emphasized each step as if to demonstrate.

I decided to let it go. When the translator worked a little better we could small-talk. Click brought me to a fissure in the rock and slipped inside. I was too large to fit, so I waited. He returned with a four handfuls of minerals. They sparkled in the moist air.

He placed them in the bent Y pattern and then added a short arm on either side. Now it looked like a bent Y overlapping a T.

"For the steam," he said. "When you wash." He gestured to my feet.

I picked up one of minerals. "Do I use this when I bathe?" I asked.

He tasted the air. "When you wash the feet." He jerked his lower hands over my feet doing a crude imitation of the ceremony I'd performed earlier.

"Oh." I laughed. "I washed the feet because it is Holy Thursday." Or at least if I were following the calendar our time it would be. I'd lost track of what day it was in real time. "Jesus washed the feet of his apostles. It's a way to show we're equal. I will perform another ceremony tomorrow for Good Friday."

"We will not be equal tomorrow?"

"No. I mean that I wish to show you more of our customs. I hope to learn some of yours too." It hit me with surprise that I meant it. "For example, what does this symbol mean?" I gestured to the minerals.

"For the steam." He slid the rocks to me. "We will be equal tomorrow."

He retreated into his fissure and when a long time passed I realized he would not be coming back. Scooping up the offered rocks, I continued on my stroll. I rather liked speaking to him and wondered what the steam and rock had to do with washing feet. The symbol had to have a special meaning as well. I'd seen it enough throughout my walk.

I wove my way through the rock village back to camp. I passed Captain Williams speaking to someone via her earpiece. She gave a curt wave and I smiled in return. She could be cordial and she was always professional, even if we disagreed on a number of religious topics.

The captain turned away and continued to speak. "The dome is stabilized and we'll be moving the majority of the supplies within the hour. We can move the teams in tomorrow afternoon."

I usually didn't eavesdrop, but I sighed in relief at the news. The planet's heat and humidity were taxing, and having the dome in place meant we'd have a sanctuary from the atmospheric conditions.

Inside the main tent, I unloaded my knapsack near my designated personal area. I was not the last to return. Dr. Sanchez and one of the language programmers, I'd learned his name was Paul, were engrossed in conversation, bent over a collection of shaped rock, turning it over, and discussing it with intense interest.

Dr. Sanchez broke from the spell first when I walked by. "Reverend! How was your day? Did you speak with any of the Kauslings?"

"Kauslings?" I smiled. I thought of Click. The name did fit better. "Yes." I wanted to tell Lena about the encounter, but decided to keep my summary brief. The day had been long and I was tired. There was no way to be sure it was the same Kausling we'd seen on the first day. "I did a short sermon and then took a stroll through the rocks. It was very educational."

Paul gestured to my language translator. "Did it give you any trouble? We seem to have hit a plateau. It happens sometimes. The translator can only decode so much, and Kauslings are less developed in communication."

"That's not true," Dr. Sanchez shot him a shocked look. "They're very advanced in communication, just not with outsiders." She glanced at me. "They have small family groups and they are able to communicate in a more intimate level among members of their collective." She glared at Paul. "Just because they don't talk to us doesn't mean they're not advanced."

Paul pressed his lips together. "That's not what I meant." He set the rock they had been studying on the mat. "I'm going to go check in with Dr. Beckermann."

The tent flapped behind him as he left.

Her eyes widened. "Did I say something wrong?"

"It's probably just the heat and gravity." I reassured her. "Have you gathered any more information on the glyphs, Dr. Sanchez?"

She waved her hand. "Call me Lena. We're friends now right? And no." She slumped in her chair and crossed her arms. "Am I going crazy? The other researchers think it's all a coincidence. That I'm reading tea leaves."

She shook her head as if she could erase the idea from her mind, but I could see in her eyes she remained convinced the translations were special. I knew how she felt, I felt it too—

this discovery had reinforced my faith. I could just imagine what it would do to someone who didn't believe. In faith, we ask people to believe in the impossible based on very few facts. What if we could provide facts? What if we could confirm the impossible?

I placed my hand over hers. "Go with your gut instinct. That is God speaking to you on what is right. He would never have shown you these things without a purpose, even if we don't know what the purpose is yet."

"But nobody else sees it!" She turned off her tablet and pushed it away.

"Blessed are they that have not seen, and yet have believed," I quoted.

"Doubting Thomas. You talked about him a few days ago." She smiled and picked at a thread on her tablet case.

"John 20:29."

"Speaking of Doubting Thomas." Her eyes motioned to the corner of the tent where Captain Williams sat. "I wonder what it must feel like to have all the answers. To have no room for doubt where faith could creep in."

I took a sip. "We all have our vices, but Jesus once told his disciples that as long as a man does good we cannot judge him. Even if he does not believe. The disciples said, If he is not one of us, he cannot do good. And Jesus corrected them, Do not hinder him, he said. Let him do good. Captain Williams means to do good, so we let her."

Lena's eyes never left the captain. "Maybe she's bitter." Lena absently stroked her arms as if she were chilled. "It must be lonely. She must have traveled thousands of light years. Everyone she knew on Earth is dead." Her eyes reddened from unshed tears. "Did you feel it?" She wiped at her eyes and tore her focus from the captain to me. "The moment we hit light speed and everyone we ever knew had lived their lives and died? Did you feel that moment where all that was left of your time was you?"

I reached for her hand again, squeezed it tight. "Be strong and courageous. Do not fear or be in dread of them, for it is the Lord your God who goes with you. He will not leave you or forsake you." Then after I whispered the section of the Bible I'd quoted, I added, "Never forget that even when God's only son lay on the cross that He did not abandon him. God is with you always, so you'll never be lonely."

I offered her these words of comfort as if it were a reflex. I watched the tension ease from her body and we carried on with light discussion.

But I had felt it, that moment where the world I knew disappeared. However, it wasn't when we hit light speed travel. I'd felt it a year before. I'd felt it in the last moments of Amelia's life. Everything I'd ever known had died in that moment on Earth.

After Lena left, I watched the captain while she stared at the dark foggy horizon through the window. We all had something in common now. We all were lonely. I clutched my Bible. Only some of us were lonelier than others.

I held a sermon the next morning, but couldn't tell if Click was in attendance. I read the story of Jonah and the Whale. I picked the stories in the bible that I thought the natives would most likely connect with—although it felt scattered, it seemed the best way to build interest. Most of the participants stayed for fifteen minutes. I drew the "Y" symbol in the dirt, asking if any of them could explain it to me. They all gathered around, clicking and chattering, nothing that my translator could pick up. Their sounds hissed through the translator. When they silenced, looking at me with some great expectation, I didn't know what to do, so I started a new story. The last of the group walked away a few minutes later. None of them stayed to hear the end of the tale.

I decided to pack up early and prepare to move my personal items to the dome. I remembered Captain Williams' conversation yesterday about the dome being ready to move into this afternoon.

I found Lena in the rec tent bent over a broken clay stick. "Hello Reverend. Have you seen Ira? We collected some interesting samples from the neighboring village on the plains today. He found this." She handed over her magnifying instrument.

"It looks like a twig covered in mud." I handed back her magnifying instrument.

"Or it could be a tool, an eating utensil, or a work of art." She ticked off each item, her face lit up with possibility.

"Or Ira found a twig that was covered in mud."

"But as a scientist you have to look at all the possible angles." She sat up in her chair and pointed at the rocks on the table a few feet away. "For example, I collected some of these tools this morning. At first I thought the natives used the tools to mash the sticky weed plants, so they could eat them as food, so I collected a few and didn't look into it further until I became captivated by some of the stone carvings. They're amazing." She pantomimed a figure with her hands, her face scrunched in concentration as if she were trying to figure the words to explain. "Have you seen the carvings?"

"No. I only ventured as far as this small village. I haven't been beyond The Steam Fields. Maybe later in the week I'll take a trip into the more populated areas."

"Well, they're marvelous, spectacular—I don't I have words to do them justice. I hope to get permission to inspect them more closely. Anyway, it seems they're grinding the sticky weed as some sort of corrosive element. If I hadn't seen them do it, I wouldn't have known. The plant makes it easier for them to carve the stones. It appeared they were eating it, but it has to go through their digestive tract as part of the process."

I cringed. "Sounds lovely."

She giggled low in her throat. "It's worse than it sounds. I edited some of it for you, but it's a different world with different values and traditions. We must seem pretty strange to them."

I thought of the foot washing ceremony yesterday and wondered how well it went over. Click appeared interested.

He even wanted an encore. "My experience so far suggests they're equally curious about us."

"Oh? So you did speak with some of the Kauslings? You've had more success than us."

"Just one fellow," I said. "I think he will meet with me tomorrow."

"I don't understand this village in The Fields," she said. "They have a more advanced gathering in the other cities farther out. They have tools, adequate food, water, less danger... why do these guys choose to live out here in The Steam Fields?"

Ira stomped into the tent and wiped his hand across his sweat-soaked shirt. "I hate this damn place." He fingered the oxygen tube. "I can't wait to take this nuisance off as well. Where's the dome? They said we would move in by the end of today." Even though Ira was a few years from being a cranky old man, he did a decent impression.

"Patience," I said. I thought to relay the information I'd overheard, but didn't want to spread something I hadn't heard first hand. "I've prayed to God and he assures me we can move into the dome within the hour."

"Oh?" Ira smirked at my joke. "And have him order us a round of burgers and beer while he's at it."

Everyone within hearing distance chuckled. But when Captain Williams announced the dome was ready for us to move into within the hour, the laughing stopped.

"The power of prayer, my friends," I said, keeping my prior knowledge from eavesdropping on the captain secret.

I gathered my things and trekked up the hill to an air-conditioned section of the dome. I'd grown used to luxury. I was not ashamed to admit it. I glanced toward Ira and his crew as they settled into their rooms. I had trouble locating mine and stopped a ship's worker to ask. He led me to a closet with a cot.

Ira appeared as I was squeezing into my space. "Nice room," he commented.

"Not exactly what I had in mind, but I don't need much, just a place to lay my head."

"Keep telling yourself that when you have a stiff neck tomorrow. Maybe you should pray for a miracle upgrade." His lips turned up into a devilish grin.

"I think I'll pray for your soul instead."

He laughed all the way back to his quarters.

I awoke the next day with a mild headache and the stiff neck Ira had prophesized. The miracle, however, was that the museum crew had left for the day and I could recover in solitude. After a cup of tea and a few muscle relaxers it was as if the entire experience was a bad memory. I gathered a few supplies and strolled down to The Steam Fields. A series of lights had been erected along the path, so at least I didn't have to strain too hard in the night vision goggles.

A few days ago I had performed a Last Supper service, although it technically was not the Lent season on Earth. Click had displayed interest in the ceremony. I chose another ceremony for today called the Stations of the Cross, which detailed the death of Jesus Christ.

I loaded the program and set the tablet on the rock I'd used as an altar. The images of Jesus carrying the cross projected on the surfaces around me. I'd chosen a recent collection of oil paintings that had been commissioned by the Church in Chile, for one reason. I knelt at the sixth painting that had captivated me, a depiction of St. Veronica wiping Christ's face with her veil. Covered in robes, her expression is that of concern and the sorrow and her eyes speak of a secret horror.

In that look I saw something I recognized only once before. I'd held Amelia's hand in her final hours. The doctors said to watch for the signs "the end was near." Fitting they put it that way, it certainly felt like the end to me—the end of everything worth living for. I rambled through life, searching for a place to belong until I met her, then I knew. Then, like a cog in a clock, everything fit into place and time began. What does a man do when he's served his purpose?

I prayed to God in her last moments to show some mercy and just before she died her tension eased and she looked at me with such peace. I knew He'd answered me. People ask how I can be so sure God exists and my response is: how could He not? When I've gazed into the eyes of the first moments in life and the last, I see Him there.

I placed my hand on Veronica's profile, wishing I could turn her attention to me. The shape of her painted face was the same as Amelia's.

I didn't have much time to ponder or fixate on the paintings, because a few Kauslings gathered and flicked their tongues at the pictures. I'd forgotten to ask Lena how much they could see. I'd read they could decipher some visual stimuli, basic shapes, and darks and lights, but was unsure how much of the pictures they could process.

Yesterday, the group who'd accumulated had a short attention span, so today I walked from group to group explaining the pictures if I noticed them taking an interest in a particular image.

The groups clumped together, huddled and caressed one another freely, sometimes nearly climbing over one other. But each cluster of Kauslings ignored the other groups. I wondered if this was discrimination amongst the collective or if the two main groups who'd arrived were from separate groups.

"This is a representation of Solomon carrying the cross for Jesus." I explained to a few of the attendees.

A commotion broke out near the final picture, the one where Jesus rose from tomb.

"It was a miracle," I explained. "He was a very special man. Someone who wanted to bring peace on Earth and he died for our sins." I hoped the translation would make sense.

"For the steam." I heard a voice crackle on the translation and I searched around for who had spoken. Except a cacophony of voices chimed, "For the steam! It is the steam!"

"Not exactly." Not at all, but we had to start somewhere. The Holy Spirit in the picture did look like a steamy cloud. "His spirit rose to the heavens and he sits by the right hand of God. He will judge us in our final days."

"He washes the feet. We are equal." This time I recognized the voice. Click stepped closer to me. His multicolored shell reflected like oil against the light of candle.

The others flicked their tongues at Click. A group walked away as if I had run out of refreshments and the party was over.

"Hello, good friend!" I greeted Click and motioned for him to come closer. I dipped the bowl in the water near one of the bubbling springs, set the minerals he'd given me inside. "I know you found this interesting the other day. I thought I'd tell the story behind it."

Without warning Click splashed his lower pincher into the water and swished it around.

I jerked back. "Whoa, I'm glad you're enthusiastic about this." I reached in and gently cupped some water in my glove and ran it over his claw.

He stilled, even his tongue ceased to dart out. When I was done he cupped the water in his claw and poured it over my hands.

"We are equal," he said.

I didn't have the heart to tell him that it was not the way the ceremony was conducted, but I did appreciate the sentiment. He tipped the bowl, spilling the water and plucked the minerals from the ground arranging them in the strange barbed "Y" symbol.

The others in the group crowded around Click and admired the symbol. Then they shuffled off showing no interest in the paintings. Click stayed behind and watched me as I cleaned and picked up the items. I placed them in my pack to haul to the dome.

"Would you like to come with me? Nobody is at the dome this time of day, but later I know there are many who would like to speak with you."

Click didn't answer, just followed behind me as he'd done yesterday. I thought about Lena's explanation of the social structure. The other locals I'd seen always traveled in groups; I'd only ever seen Click alone. Where was Click's collective?

We reached the dome and Click didn't approach with me, which was probably best. I didn't think the extra oxygen would be healthy for him any more than the extra gases in his air were good for humans. I did a quick check for Lena or Ira, but neither was inside.

I hurried back to Click, worried he would go home and I'd have to wait to see him again. I wanted to speak with him, wondering what he thought of the Stations of the Cross.

"How did you like the sermon, the stories from my world?"

Click snapped his lower claws in a rapid succession. "Stories of your great man?"

"Yes. We call him Jesus Christ. He was the son of God."

Click didn't respond. His feet made little steps in place.

"We are trying to find out more about your people. I learned you communicate in groups. I think this is why it's harder to communicate between our people and yours. Can you communicate better between collectives?"

"No. Collectives do not communicate."

"So they don't communicate much between each other...or they don't communicate within the collective?

There was a long pause, then, "I don't understand."

"It seems that people from your world form groups. We call them collectives. And you talk to your group, but the groups don't look like they talk much to other groups."

"There is one."

"There is one collective?"

He gestured to my translator. "There is one."

"Is there someone here who can communicate to all the collectives?" It made sense, sort of like a queen bee. Click wobbled his feet, which I'd learned was the equivalent of a head nod. "Can you take me to this person?"

"I do not understand," Click said.

I sighed. It was too much to hope for an easy solution to our communication problems.

"I will show you things," he said after a while. "You will understand. There is only one."

"That sounds wonderful!" I spoke a little too loud and he shivered in response. "Oh, sorry." I whispered. "I'd love to see more of your world."

"I will show you the steam." He dug his claws into the side of a rock and hoisted his body along the cracks and fissures. In a matter of minutes he had climbed several feet.

I tested the rock, unsure of my climbing abilities. "I don't know if I can climb this." I called to him, but he'd already gone a significant distance and apparently hadn't noticed I wasn't following. I quickly scanned the area and saw a few steep rocks along the side I could use as steps for a short distance. After I reached the plateau, I slowly swung around the opposite side. Climbing in heavier gravity proved difficult. Even though it would take longer to reach the top, at least this path was physically possible.

Since the planet was larger than Earth I could see much farther and at this higher elevation the horizon appeared to span for miles. The dim light from a distant sun cast shadows along the bowl shaped valley, and the Steam Fields nestled in the center. Tufts of steam floated into the air like chimney smoke. Little vegetation grew in the fields—only small croppings of twisting vine-like weeds. The land beyond had rolling brown grasses and short, stubby bush trees. A little village of scattered rock huts jutted from the grasses about ten miles away. I understood what Lena had said. The village did appear more civilized. The Steam Fields were desolate in comparison. It was as if a hand had scooped the valley dry, leaving anthill-like structures scattered in a broken line along the center.

Deep, riverless canyons spread out like fingers reaching toward the village. I could see figures the size of the local inhabitants, but they didn't move. Perhaps Lena's statues? But at this angle I couldn't tell.

I skirted around the lip of the ledge until I discovered an opening. My muscles ached; it would still be a few days until I acclimated to the gravity. The amount of walking, the extra strain in my body, and the food rations since I'd embarked on my mission made my clothes sag more each day.

"Click!" I yelled. Then remembering he didn't react well to loud sounds I lowered my voice "Click, I took another path up the hill. I don't have the ability to climb like you."

I heard scraping, a rock on rock clink, followed by another. I walked in the direction of the sound and found Click bent over a pile of jagged stones next to a fissure that steamed and bubbled. He secured a stone in his claw and chipped at an embedded mineral. I picked a stone from the pile and lowered myself to a spot of dry ground. I aimed for grace, but instead collapsed. My muscles were weak from the climb.

The stones made for a lumpy backrest and I hooked my arm on the pile, holding the stone to the thin light streaming through the heavy clouds. The rock was some sort of sedimentary formation, probably formed from thousands of years of mudslides and volcanic activity.

"You know—" I started and set the stone down and picked another for inspection. "For a while, on the planet I'm from, I used to collect all kinds of rock and crystals. I'd always meant to take a class, learn a little more about the geology of the area." But then I got interested in cave spelunking, discovered I was claustrophobic, and moved on to another hobby.

He paused his chipping. "You are of the steam?"

I twisted around to glance at the steam vent. "I, uh, no. I'm of the planet Earth."

He resumed his work. "You communicate to all collectives."

I fingered my translator. "Well, it's a machine that helps me to communicate."

"All the visitors have the machine," he said.

"They do." I sat straighter, pulled my legs into a different position when my toes tingled. "In fact, the other visitors would like to speak with you. They've had trouble talking to the others on your planet. Our people are interested in your people."

"Yes," he said and the mineral snapped loose, falling with solid thunk, thunk, thunks to the ground. Click seized the mineral and cradled it close to his body.

"Maybe after we're done here I can take you to meet with Lena and Ira. They're my friends and would like to speak to you. The captain may have others, too. But if you're uncomfortable in any way I'll walk you to your home. Is there anyone else, maybe someone in your collective who would be interested in joining us?"

"No," he said and looked meaningfully at the mineral cupped in his upper hands.

"Well, perhaps if I meet them I can speak to them."

"I show you collectives tomorrow." He waddled to the fissure, paced around the steaming spout. "Today I will show you steam." He held the mineral over the steam and plunked it in the hole. The steam's color changed from a sulfuric yellow to a lime greenish.

I was about to comment, when Click reached to his leg and dug at the exoskeleton and pulled off a bit of scaly tissue and placed it in the hole. I now knew where his scars came from. He looked at me expectantly. Did he want me to do the same? I imagined myself tearing a piece of skin and cringed.

"I don't think I should. I could get an infection, or a burn. Your water is more acidic..." I tried to think of how to say it so he'd understand.

"You're of the steam. Your great man gave his blood." He claws clicked and his tongue darted he looked to the sky as if trying to remember. "For this is my blood."

My heart beat faster. He'd remembered the words from the Last Supper reading. Mathew 26:28. "Listen, Click. It's not a literal thing. We don't have to actually give our blood."

His tongue continued to explore the air, like he was checking for my authenticity. He thrust his arms out. "This is the steam. You are not of the steam? Your great man is not of the steam?" Then he turned away and lowered his head, thinking.

"I don't know what is going on here. It's hard to communicate with the language translator not working the way it was intended, but people are working on the software."

He flipped around. "Can you see the steam?"

I held out my arms and gestured to the steam. "Yes. It's sort of hard to miss."

He hobbled around me and pointed to the horizon. "Can you see the other steam from the other collectives? Can you see the steam of before?"

"I think I'm not quite following what exactly steam is? I see water vapor. Am I missing something?"

He tapped on my knapsack where I kept my Bible. "Your great man, he could see. He can connect to all the collectives."

"We don't have collectives on our planet. We can all speak to each other openly. We can communicate outside of our family as long as we can speak the language and even then we have these." I motioned to the translator.

He ignored me and picked through the rock. "He is of the steam."

I sighed. "Jesus is of our planet. Sent by God, His only son, and he died for our sins. I think I can explain—"

"No." Click arranged the rocks on the ground, the Y overlapping a T. "He came of the steam. He rose from the steam."

"He was born from a virgin, conceived by the Holy Ghost. I guess that could be kind of like steam." I flipped though the pages to find some pictures. I could explain myself better with pictures.

"He communicates to all the collectives." Click practically vibrated now. He was clearly upset.

"Our translators help us with that." I closed the book. "Maybe if we go back to the dome and speak to Ira and Lena they can help us figure this out."

Click kicked at the rocks and a section gave away. "There is only one."

"Okay. Let's take a minute." I breathed in and out, demonstrating how to calm down.

Click's tongue flickered rapidly, until his shoulders lowered and he seemed to calm. Then he bent and gathered a handful of minerals and hobbled to the side of the rock.

"That's right," I said. "We should go to Ira. He's really good at this sort of thing."

"There is only one," Click said again, this time with less anger in his posture. He swung his foot over the edge and his claws acted as pickaxes lowering himself down the steep hill.

"Jesus was the only son of God—"

He didn't break his stride and repeated, "Only one."

I eyed the slope of the hill and visualized myself tumbling down. I might even take out Click on the way like a Jack and an extraterrestrial Jill.

"I'm going down the way I came up. I'll meet you down there," I called out.

On the way down I replayed the conversation and Click's words took shape. It was clear he was not speaking about Jesus. But he did take interest in the stories from the Bible. He spoke of the steam as if it were some sort of spiritual symbol; could there be a connection amongst his collective? I wondered: maybe if I could speak to other members of his group, we might be able to clarify this misunderstanding.

My feet found a stable shelf to rest and I took a deep breath. I'd taken a different direction to descend the hill and had a better view of The Steam Fields crater below. I could see the canyons now and verified that the figures in the distance must be some sort of statues clustered in the widest gulch.

But that wasn't the sight that froze me in place or had me squinting and risking my life to get a better look. No, the sight to behold was the stone in the shape of the Y overlapping T on the grassy plains over looking the gorge. Strings and clumps of debris flapped in the gentle breeze around the stone structure.

I wished I'd brought at least my tablet. Then I could capture an image and enhance the picture for more detail. I strained for a while longer, until I admitted there was no safe passage to get a better view. After I met Click below and took him to Lena and Ira I would go explore the gorge.

If there was a sort of primitive religion on the planet the researchers had missed, I wanted to have knowledge of it. If a religion already existed, even a weak one, I'd need to detail it in my report to the church. Our focus was not to erase existing beliefs, but to add and enrich. The cultures may even have tidbits of knowledge that could benefit Christianity; just as the artifacts and glyphs on Astik that Lena had been so fascinated by, which had led many into believing in the possibility of God.

I poked my way around the hill, sliding and skidding, gripping and praying all the way to the bottom. But like a magnet, whenever I paused for breath I found myself turned in the direction of the symbol on the plain, wondering.

I reached the bottom of the hill and Click was not in sight. I trekked to the dome and Ira and Lena hadn't seen him either. They offered to accompany me to search for him, but I thought their presence would frighten Click and so I begged off their offers and went to find him.

Every fissure seemed the same as the last. When I came to the one I thought was Click's, a pair of foreign ghostly white eyes peeked back at me, and a curious flicking tongue, but they were not Click's. Through my interactions with Click I had begun to notice subtle differences among the species; wider set eyes, thicker legs or arms, variations of patterns in the exoskeletons. I knew I'd be able to spot Click in a crowd and I didn't see him all afternoon. I returned to the dome empty-handed and my promise to explore the gorge postponed.

I set up my sermon the next day—a simple reading of the Tower of Babel. The story reminded me of the collective groups on Kaus, and I hoped it would spark some interest among the crowd. With the growing curiosity among the group, I hoped I could build on that sentiment and get a discussion going. I projected some drawings of the event along the rock surfaces, but none of the Kauslings took any notice. Desperate, I pulled out the water bowl from before, but nobody ventured forward. They moved along the scene without even a glance in the direction of the altar.

I could swear as one group passed I heard a whisper in the translator: "Not the one." But it was crackly and faded. I must have misheard.

Again I spent the rest of the afternoon and evening searching for Click, only to end the day disappointed.

"Maybe he's just off on some errand," Lena offered that evening while I played a round of chess with Ira. "Could he be under the weather?"

Ira positioned his rook to threaten my queen. "I think you offended him. You should have given him a hunk of flesh for his ceremony."

I blinked at the mess on the board and how I'd get myself out of peril, then leaned back in my chair rubbed my eyes. "I didn't want to open myself up to infection, alien disease—"

"Think of it as a sacrifice in the name of God." I didn't have to peer though my fingers to see the joking grin on Ira's face; I could hear it loud and clear in his tone.

"Oh for heaven's sake. This is going to bother me all night." Lena swooped to the board and used my knight to seize Ira's queen.

"Cheating!" Ira pointed at Lena and frowned. "She's cheating. You can't let her cheat like that." He reached across the table and smacked my leg. "Tell her she's going to hell."

"I most certainly will not go to hell," Lena shouldered her equipment and brushed off her pants. "I'm going to bed. You can lose on your own. Gentlemen." She nodded at us both and crossed her arms before marching away.

When she was gone, he returned the queen and knight into place. "Pretend you never saw that."

I stared off into the distance, thinking.

"Bah." He swiped the entire board clean. "She totally ruined the whole game." He programed the tablet for a new game.

"Do you really think I might have offended Click?"

"I have no idea." He fiddled with the games program, gliding though the various options. He didn't glance my way while he searched. "Should I be looking for solitaire games?"

"I think you're right. I offended him."

He turned off the program and crossed his legs with a huff. "Yeah, I'm sure you did. Aliens have feelings too you know. I've been studying their customs and it seems that within the collectives they have some sort of telepathy. It explains why we're having difficulty communicating." He ran his hands through his hair. "Hey, look. We've had minimal luck on this expedition talking with the locals and setting up a trade. I think you have a knack for talking to people and aliens. Why don't you come with us tomorrow and we'll help you with your problem. *Quid pro quo* and all that."

"Lena mentioned a group of statues. I'd like to see them. Can we get up close?"

"We've been going the respectful route for a week now and it's done us no good. When they invited us here they told us to go and touch whatever we liked. It seems their culture is very open." A grin I could only associate with trouble crept on his face. "Let's test that tomorrow."

I nodded and a quiver of excitement shot though my system. Not quite a deal with the devil, but close enough.

I inspected the fraying edges of my shirt and Ira didn't question me again. He loaded a solitary game. After a few hours I sat alone.

Thoughts of the gorge and its connection to Click's spiritual steam references filled my mind. If I could get more information, maybe it would lead to finding Click. Tomorrow, I vowed, I wouldn't hold a sermon. I would go to the gorge to find clues.

Lena, Ira, and I made it as far as the edge of the village before Captain Williams stopped us and ordered us to return to the dome for safety equipment.

"The scientists who've surveyed that area say it's unstable. Possible rock slides. I won't allow anyone from the teams to enter without precautions," Williams said.

After the short stutter-start we returned a few hours behind our intended schedule, but properly prepared with extra oxygen, climbing hooks, flares, and a full day's provisions. It felt a little like bringing a carnival to a birthday party, but I would hate to be stuck in a situation that would prove Captain Williams right.

We passed a number of caves with water dripping from mineral formations at the openings. The sounds of trickling, bubbling, and occasional rumbling were constant. At one point, Lena and Ira engaged in a long discussion about the early data on the cultural habits of Raymon V, a planet we were scheduled to visit next after our decade here. I slowed my pace, allowing them to speed ahead, and while drinking from my canteen I swore I heard the unmistakable crunch of clawed feet on gravel, but when I searched, there was nothing.

Stacks of boulders, piles of rocks, and a line of stones four feet high blocked our entrance into the gorge. High enough to keep out the natives, but not a challenge for us.

"We could climb over it," Lena explained. "When we first came across it, we were on our way to the village on the plains above the fields, but we decided against causing any disputes. I mean, why would they fence it off?"

I propped my elbows on the wall to catch my breath. From here the sculptures were exquisite. Realistic craftsmanship and detail. The statues were encrusted with milky colored gems.

Ira stepped onto the wall and carefully placed his feet to hop over. "Maybe we're thinking too much like humans. We think walls are to keep something in or something out, but walls might have a different purpose to the Kauslings. They've made it clear we can explore anything we like. If we're not supposed to be here I expect we'll find out soon enough."

Lena shrugged and started to climb. "Better to ask for forgiveness than permission." She twisted around to face me. "Are you coming?"

I slid my arms from their perch. "Of course."

Even though Ira had a head start, it was Lena who made it over the wall first. Although she cautioned us several times about being careful in the heavy gravity while pausing to suck in extra air from her oxygen mask. Ira managed a close second with one "Goddamnit" that he instantly retracted when I glared at him. My two companions waited semi-patiently for me to maneuver the wall, before giving up and surveying the surrounding area I heaved my leg over the top section of boulders. Ira scraped at the gorge wall noting the various mineral deposits on his tablet.

I made it past the highest point of the wall and attempted to secure my footing, wind-milling my arms a few times to regain my balance.

Ira tilted his screen for Lena to see. "The grooves and mineral deposits indicate volcanic activity and flooding occurred here about five hundred years ago."

I joined them, brushing off the dust from my suit. "I read in the geography bulletin that The Steam Fields were created through multiple volcanic eruptions over time and the crater was formed from an extinct volcano."

"We've surveyed the aqueducts," Lena added. "The Kauslings have a system for pumping liquid from the crater to prevent the Steam Fields from becoming a lake. I assumed because they have an established village, that the species doesn't migrate much. They've shown tendencies to rebuild rather than move to a more hospitable area."

I inspected the wall, running my finger along the textured rock. "What are these grooves?"

"Dig marks," Ira said. "They've been digging this section out for centuries."

I touched the hash marks with more reverence and awe. The determination of the Kauslings to create such a space was astounding, but for what purpose? My gut told me it was related to their spiritual beliefs in the steam. And the strange symbol on the cliffs of the plains above.

Lena made a few notes on her tablet before placing it in her bag. "And then placed the statues inside, I'm assuming."

We walked into the gorge where a few of the Kauslings were moving rock, placing a paste-like substance on the statues, and carving. The carvings depicted Kauslings to exact scale, and the patterns in their exoskeleton appeared to have been painted with mud of various shades of red. Some were missing portions of limbs, or broken sections. I inched closer to one damaged statue. The inhabitants were cleaning a section of a large boulder farther down the gorge and didn't acknowledge me, so I ran my hand along the slope of the stone figure's outstretched arm.

Whoever it was he seemed to be reaching out, his head angled high. From a distance it seemed like a position of prayer to the heavens, but at a closer angle the body was stretched as if to be reaching for something in a desperate plea.

I scanned the other formations and instead of seeing art I saw a scene laced in horror. Limbs torn, claws covering faces, one in the center rolled in a ball and one toward the back of a group huddled as if taking shelter against a gruesome storm. I jogged to the back of the gorge where the workers crowded together on the largest boulder, passing Ira on my way.

Ira crouched beside one of the alien statues and scanned a section with a sensor. The largest of the statues seemed to be a incised with a tangle of bodies holding on to one another. The workers carved delicately around the edges of the figures.

I paused behind an alien statue whose head was partially missing. Embedded in the mineral rock I saw a section of exoskeleton. Through Ira's mask I could see his face drain of color and Lena leaned over to examine the results. Then Lena turned away from the scene, covering her face.

I didn't need to see Ira's tablet. I already knew—these weren't statues; they were petrified bodies.

This was a memorial site.

We walked away from the scene, each of us avoiding the other's gaze. I murmured prayers because I was afraid if I let the quiet between us grow my mind would flick the pictures of the event as a distorted sympathetic memory.

"How long ago?" Lena's voice cracked, hovering between a whisper and a plea. She cleared her throat. "By your calculations, I mean."

"800 Earth years..." Ira answered, a distance in his voice. "Maybe more, maybe less. This planet has the perfect conditions for the petrification process." He glanced at this tablet to verify the readings.

Lena straightened. "We should let the others know and get some samples."

Lena and Ira were scientists, so explanations and test samples crept in place of their emotions. Rationalizing. It was how they coped. I, however, prayed.

We spent three hours in the village. My body, although somewhat acclimated to the gravity, still dragged and felt heavy. We split up. Lena and Ira moved along to another part of the village, but I hung back, telling them I'd catch a ride with the last rover shuttle to the dome.

But I didn't stay in the town. I headed for the plains and toward the barbed "Y" symbol.

When I heard the ticking of claws behind me, I knew I'd been followed. Except this time I was sure of my shadow. When I faced Click, he didn't hide or cower from me.

"You followed me to the statues. Do you know what happened to them?" I asked.

"Taken by the steam," he said.

"So terribly sad." I shook my head, my heart filled with sorrow for the ancient tragedy.

"Warned," Click said as he motioned at my translator. "The mud was coming." And his arms flapped around wildly as if reenacting the event.

"Someone warned them to leave and they chose to stay?"

He settled. "Yes."

"Who warned them?"

"Of the steam."

"The water vapor? I'm having trouble understanding the significance of the steam. Is it important to you?"

"Yes."

"Was it the water vapor? Or was it a being?"

Click lowered his head, his claws clicked together rapidly as if he were thinking of what to say and then he pointed to the symbol ahead. "Only one. A great one."

I scratched my chin and tried to put all the pieces together. "When you said that to me the first time, it was when I asked you about how the collective communicates. I understood that it was within the collective, and external communication was minimal. You said there was 'only one' and I guessed that there was someone who could communicate with all the collectives. Does this great one live near this symbol on the plains?"

Click's tongue flicked like a heartbeat and glanced to the formation ahead. "He is of the steam."

Click must be speaking of a being, one of his species. I ran though the possible ideas of what he could mean while we walked. A breeze blew at us from behind, pushing us forward. I quizzed him on all the possible meanings.

Is the steam a sort of purification? Yes.

Is the vapor that raises out of the rocks the steam? Yes.

Does everyone in his village believe in the steam? Yes.

When people die to they go to the steam? Yes.

So the steam had several meanings. Was the steam a sort of heaven to them? A connection between collectives, when no other appeared to exist?

The details of the formation grew more visible the closer we got. I could see the rocks had been carved in a particular shape and debris caught in wedges on either side. We approached the figures from the back. A breeze whipped around the formation creating a low tonal hum.

My head filled with questions that I hoped would soon be answered. Click pecked at the pile of rocks, checking them for security, and then began to climb. I walked around the base, too tired to go much further.

"Click?" I asked while he was still in hearing range, "Where is your collective?"

He stopped climbing, his body perched on the edge of a flat rock. "They are gone. I have none."

His answer hit me in the center of my chest, a deep ache, but somehow I knew. I'd felt a connection to Click. We were kindred spirits—alone in a universe where everyone seemed to have someone.

He climbed and I skirted around the base of the pile of rocks. Click reached his destination and instead of facing the large Y formation, he angled out toward the plains. He stretched his arms wide.

"There is one," he said. "He is of the steam." Then he lowered his head and remained motionless.

I hurried around to the front, tripped over a few rocks along the way. I stumbled and caught myself before my knee crashed down on a jagged rock. When I glanced up before I righted myself and froze.

From where I knelt, Click's outstretched arms aligned perfectly with the Y rock, even his smaller lower arms lined up with the barbs coming out below the Y. But that was not what caused my heart to pound, my palms to sweat, my fingers to lose their grip on my bag. My Bible tumbled across the pebbles.

Behind Click on the rock, it was not debris that flapped in the wind, but remains. Half buried in the rock was the body of another Kausling. The arms hung limp and the skeleton dangled precariously. It was as if the skeleton were a bug pinned and prepared for examination. Parts of the skull had decayed, but the rest of the exoskeleton remained intact enough to verify what had happened.

"What happened to him?" I asked.

"He was a great man," he said, and his use of the word 'man' startled me until I realized it would be the only word the translator had used for "being" and since all the great people I'd mentioned were men, Click only knew to use that word. "He saved many, but was killed because they didn't understand. He was all collectives."

The position of the body, the way the rock dipped where its arms once had been secured, the angle its head hung—indicated it had not been a victim of the disaster in the canyon. Click explained this poor soul had been crucified.

I thought of Lena's glyphs on Astik and the savior mentioned in an extinct culture.

"I think I'm beginning to understand." I scooped my Bible from the rocks and set it aside. "Tell me more about your great one."

※

Report
Kaus 12TV7

I think I made a mistake agreeing to work as a missionary on this planet. Perhaps it was my waning belief in God, my grief for my wife, or homesickness. In any case, I never thought I'd doubt the teaching of the church.

I came to teach about Jesus, our savior, only to find one already existed on Kaus. And he or she is every bit as important as Jesus. I'm still uncovering all the stories from the local population. Furthermore, anthropologists stationed on this planet (See Museum Project Reports Kaus Beckermann/Sanchez 7558, 8742, 9047, and others) have received similar reports from other areas of the planet and surrounding worlds which closely resemble a variety of Terran religions: Islam, Buddhism, Taoism...the list goes on. There are even sects which don't believe in a greater power at all and rely on science for answers. After all, throughout Earth history several stories in the Bible were similar to other religions and cultures, but I never imagined the phenomena would spread beyond our planet. Is it one big coincidence? I think it depends on your perspective and I'm slowly accepting that perspective in broader terms for the first time in my life.

Regardless, there is something at work here we don't fully understand. I hope this report finds you well.

God Bless.

INCI

Book Two

Dead Prophets

TINA GOWER

Thomas Inkle didn't intend to work through the weekend. He had planned it all out. He was going to book a cruise with the last of his savings. He licked his lips and swore he could already taste the halibut. Those weeks of accrued vacation? He'd finally do it and use them all to himself.

Himself and Anita, of course. Along with three home-care nurses. A digital-neuro-bio specialist. And arrangements for special handicap accessibility.

Anita would be ecstatic. She deserved to live life to the fullest. What life she had left.

Except he would have to work through the weekend. He hadn't been told yet, but he just knew. Call it a sixth sense. Of course he could say no, but there would be no choice. He could see how it would all go down as his boss slapped on another antacid patch. Mr. Filmore already had two other patches on his right arm and had prematurely gray hair. He was technically ten years younger than Tom, but looked about ten years older. He frowned as he swiped through the channel's late night schedules.

The digital desk display glowed blue. Mr. Filmore stood between the grid and Tom's desk. Why didn't Tom sit with the other film splicers? With an open office and so many possibilities, why did Mr. Filmore choose today to stand in front of him? His boss's eyes focused on the 2:00 a.m. time slot and then his gaze narrowed on Tom.

"Tim, get over here."

"It's Tom."

Mr. Filmore waved away the correction. "I have trouble keeping you interns straight."

"I've worked here for thirty years, sir."

But Mr. Filmore didn't hear, maybe because Tom mumbled. Anita told him he needed to speak more clearly. Annunciate. Be assertive. Tom stood up straight. He towered over his boss, but then he slouched back down.

"We've had a huge set-back on the Hwain Documentary." Mr. Filmore framed his hands in front of them, spreading out his fingers, and tapping, creating a visual. The documentary played in triple time. "It's no good. It'll fit an hour time slot, but we had the time cut down to a half hour. We've got to get it down to eighteen minutes to fit the new slot."

He sent the file into Tom's digital basket by touching the thin metal band on Tom's wrist. "Also the Peace Talks on Jupiter." He shrugged and itched one of his antacid patches.

Tom fiddled with his wristband, wondering if he could ask Chon in editing to take over the job. Or maybe suggest it? Tom needed to practice turning away work when his plate was already full. Plus the cruise. Did they serve shrimp? Anita wanted shrimp. Not that she could eat it. She had been limited to liquid through her feeding tube. But she wanted the shrimp for Tom.

Mr. Filmore looked at Tom, and he realized his boss had asked him a question. "I'm sorry?"

Mr. Filmore dragged out a long disappointed sigh. Tom knew how he felt. He wanted to go on a cruise. Not just wanted, needed. He needed one last attempt to convince Anita not to leave him. She wanted to go peacefully and on her own terms. Tom wanted to give her a reason to live, and if she didn't then at least they'd have one last moment of happiness.

So yeah, Tom was disappointed, too. It was unfair. As soon as Mr. Filmore was finished he'd tell him. He'd tell his boss to find someone else.

"I said," Mr. Filmore straightened, breathing like he was asking for peace between two bickering children, "we can't have any references to anything spiritual or religious from any culture on any planet. Because of the Worlds' Peace Talks. It would be disrespectful. And this documentary is scattered with references. Even historical, factual, proven data—we can't have a reference. Not even a hint. The legislation has come down hard on media. If we slip we get slapped with a fine. It could ruin the progress made. So it should be easy to find what to edit."

His boss gave him a hard stare, waiting for a reply.

Here was his chance to refer the project to another employee. "Mr. Filmore, sir. With all due respect...and I do have considerable respect for you and this company. In my thirty years here—"

"Mr. Filmore," Jessica from accounting called from across the room. She leaned over another employee's desk that had numbers displayed in columns rising from it like skyscrapers. Several were highlighted in red. "We've got some figures that need your attention."

With that, Mr. Filmore left. Walked away without even acknowledging that Tom had been speaking to him.

"Wait! Mr. Filmore!" Tom followed, jogging behind. "I can't take this project. If you'll just give me a minute to explain." The hum of voices quieted. Heads peeked around their halo displays. Screens flickered on pause. A hushed whispering began. Or maybe Tom just imagined it all, and in a second things were back to the way they were. The buzz of voices busy working at their stations.

Jessica and Mr. Filmore pointed at the numbers, discussing. Tom hovered behind them.

When the group stopped speaking Tom jumped in. "Isn't the documentary about spiritual traditions from around the explored galaxy?"

The group ignored him. He repeated the question louder.

"Excuse me," Mr. Filmore said to the accountants. He faced Tom again.

Yes! This was it! He had his attention, now to go in for the kill. "Why not just cut the program? Put in an old clip in its spot."

"We told the shareholders we'd deliver the program. They want a show that acknowledges the spiritual differences, but doesn't give weight to any one religion. It needs to be more factual and less speculative. No references to dominant religions."

"That doesn't make any sense. What exactly am I supposed to edit?"

"You'll figure it out, Tim."

"Tom."

"Right. I need it by Monday."

"But I won't be here on Monday. I've got a vacation. I've got personal time. I'll pass this to Chon."

"Fine." He flicked his hand like he was absently tossing a piece of trash.

Mr. Filmore continued to speak with the accountants. Tom blinked in disbelief. He'd done it? He'd asserted himself? Anita was right. She would be so excited! They'd celebrate. Tom was on his way. He'd book the tickets tonight.

Tom made his way to the coveted back corner table that editing had claimed for the day, a little skip to his stride. He calibrated his work band to pass off the file as soon as he connected with Chon.

Except Chon wasn't at his desk.

"Where's Chon?" he asked Bianca.

She looked up from packing her coffee cup and data chips into her bag for the weekend. She cleared her completed files from her wristband and turned it off. "Out sick. Happened about an hour ago. Flu. Poor guy. Of all the time to have the antivirals fail."

"Who's taking his assignments?"

"We split up most of them and..." She opened a document between them and scanned the memo, "Erica took over for him."

"I need to speak to her."

"She's out, too." Bianca squeezed her hand into a fist and the documents between them vanished. "On work-from-home maternity leave. Her wife finally had the baby. He's adorable. They went with Sam for the name. I won the betting pool. Guessed the date and weight." Bianca fist pumped in the air.

"What? How can she take over for Chon? How do I get something to her?"

"Through the work-from-home data portal." She checked the clock. "Oh damn! Portal closed for the day. You'll have to check it again after the weekend."

Tom swallowed. He felt his victory evaporating. "Can you..." He held out his band.

"Sorry." She unclipped hers, shut it down.

The lights flickered, dimming to night mode. She strolled past him, spinning and walking backward through the door. "Have a good weekend, Tom. Say hi to Anita for me." She stopped, leaning against the doorframe. "I'll have to stop by this weekend. She's just across the hall and I think it's been months since I've seen her. Hey, don't you leave for your cruise soon? I think that's great that she still feels up to going out."

Anita kept the worst details from her friends and neighbors. She'd set a date two months from now to end it. Nobody knew. Nobody suspected. Nobody seemed to notice the pain she was in. Except Tom.

Tom smiled. He could feel the edges of his lips quivering. "Uh, still figuring out the details."

The office went from a boil to a mild simmer as people left for the weekend. Tom opened the file. Might as well get started. It opened with B reel scenery of twelve planets. He didn't recognize any of them, except for Kaus. Miserable darkness, through a haze of bubbling, steaming geysers. Underground tunnels where the natives lived. At least he didn't live on Kaus. Although he heard some of it was beautiful. He skipped the video ahead.

The narrator explained the Kauslings' spiritual beliefs and family hierarchy. It was all pretty fascinating. How the people communicated through an emotional hive-like collective. Of course, not a true hive, and it was somewhat offensive to say so. Maybe he could just focus on Kaus. Take out the sections that described the Kauslings, find some B-reel footage of the planet, and splice it into the documentary. He could set the scenery to music and eliminate the voice-over.

He watched the Kaus sections again, listening for any references to religion, especially the parts where the Kaus spiritual structure was described. He'd have to carefully edit those sections.

"...beliefs were held under attack. The Testament caused a mild controversy before being thrown out. The Barker Testament since then has become discredited and forgotten. A historical footnote of the dangers in blending cultures..."

The Barker Testament? Tom had never heard of it. He watched the section again. Only that one mention. No explanation. Testament sounded very much like an Earth religious reference. Probably the exact thing his boss would want edited out. He marked the time stamp on the film and moved on.

He sketched out his plan for the segment. His mind wandered back to the Testament reference. What was it? The way the narrator had said it. A controversy? He had never heard of it before.

A soft whistle echoed in the editing room. Tom jerked in his seat, glancing around. He smelled cleaning detergent and sneezed.

The janitor rolled in with a mop and chemicals. "I can go around and do the other offices if you still need time here."

Tom blinked. The clock read 9:00 p.m. He hadn't realized he'd been here for four hours beyond the time he was supposed to leave. He'd promised the day nurse he'd be there before she left for the night.

He packed up his desk. "Oh, no. I, uh, I was just leaving."

On the long elevator ride down from the office to the train platform, Tom expanded his media screen.

Barker Testament.

He scratched his chin. If it wasn't a religious reference maybe he should keep it in? He sent Anita a quick message.

On my way. Lost track of time.

<No problem. I've been up late working on my memoir. Do you think people will want to know my daily routine? I don't want

it to read like a medical journal. Whatever I do, it has to be spectacular. I want to make a difference. I don't want my death to be meaningless. >

Tom's stomach twisted whenever Anita mentioned death. Especially her own death. He didn't want to think of Anita gone. He didn't want think about being alone.

Tom's heart beat faster. His palms were slick. The burn in his lungs warned him of an anxiety attack. He breathed deeply, patting his pocket for his pills. A few spilled onto the elevator floor as the cage jolted to a stop. Tom popped a pill under his tongue.

<*Tom? Are you still there?*>

He chose his words carefully, editing and changing around the tone. The project consumed most of her time. She had a very strict deadline. She wanted the book wrapped up in a few weeks, then would spend the last weeks with friends and family. It was important to her, and he didn't want her to know about his attacks.

Whatever you do, it will be interesting. You're the first generation with Young-Radly Syndrome. Future generations will want to know the sacrifices you made so they could beat the disease.

<*It doesn't feel right. I want something that will leave a mark.*>

It wasn't fair, he wanted to type. Caring-special-positive-full-of-life Anita didn't deserve to suffer. He waited on the platform for his train and watched a group of teens. They messed with the interactive travel kiosk, causing it to blink. Above the platform another train hummed, glowing green to announce its arrival to an even higher platform. The electrical tracks crossed and stacked like a multiple freeway intersection.

The teens threw a fire popper on the ground. It hissed and sparked. Hair in messy knots (what a disgusting fad!), e-cigar sticks hung from their lips. The habit had been deemed unsafe, causing gum bleeding and lung problems. Yet here these kids were, making bad choices when Anita had no choices. She didn't have a choice when she got her diagnosis. Didn't have a choice when her neuropathways shut down. Didn't have a choice when she could no longer speak. She was confined to a wheelchair and spoke through a computer.

She just had one choice left. Suffer or die.

<What are you working on? It must be interesting if it kept you at work for so long.>

It's nothing.

There was a long pause. *<When you get home we need to go over a few details with the funeral home. They had a few follow-up questions.>*

Tom felt numb. His meds were kicking in. He didn't want to think about death. His mind grasped onto the last interesting thing he'd seen.

Hey, have you ever heard of The Barker Testament?

<No... Running a search. Found some papers. Looks like some guy who thinks he found Jesus on another planet. Weird. It says he was declared insane.>

Tom made a note to edit that reference out. A guy thinking he found Jesus would definitely qualify as displaying a dominant Earth religion. This editing piece would continue to be a burden. So much for getting his mind off depressing things.

At his apartment door he pressed his thumb into the digital lock. It buzzed. The light blinked red. He placed his thumb in a new position, trying again.

Buzz.

Red.

Damn it.

Once more, and the door opened from the other side before he could get it to scan.

Betty, the Friday evening nurse, laughed. "I always know when it's you. You need to have them check that at the front desk."

Tom scooted his bag onto the shelf by the door and hooked his coat on the wall. "I did have them check it. They said I have shallow prints."

Betty wrapped a gauzy scarf around her neck, and arranged her hat on her head. "Whatever that means."

<It means computers hate him.> Anita chimed in.

Her digital voice crackled through the speaker.

Tom unhooked a speaker cover from the wall and inspected the wires. "This damn thing. I thought I'd fixed it."

Betty shook her head. "Broke again this afternoon. Her room is clear, but out here it's static."

"We should really get someone to rewire the whole house with a better system. This one is fifteen years old."

<Tom, that's ridiculous. This one works fine for what we need. Besides you won't be needing it much longer.>

Tom's skin prickled again, but the pill kept him steady.

Betty pursed her lips, and her eyes were a mix of sad disproval and compassion. "All right, you two. Try not to get into too much trouble."

Betty updated the care records, while Tom grabbed some food. Her fingers tapped expertly on the screen. "We've already done the bath, I've hooked her ports up to her sensors in her room, and tucked in. She should get some sleep."

<I'll sleep when I feel like it. Besides, you can blame Tom for keeping me up. He's got me on an interesting research journey for his work.>

Tom bit into an apple. "The Testament thing?" he said while chewing. "I'm going to have to cut it. Don't waste your time."

Betty waved goodbye, and Tom shooed her toward the front door.

<Fine, Betty, try to sneak out without even a goodbye. You know I can read your body language on the sensor and see you inching toward the door on the neuro-monitor.>

Betty laughed. "I'd never think of it. You always like to know what's going on, even after I've put you in your room for the night. Good-bye, darling. I'll see you on Monday." She stepped into the hallway and propped the door open with her foot. She cast a questioning glance at Tom. Her eyebrows wiggled and she sailed her hand like a boat.

He shook his head.

She frowned. Her shoulders slumped. "I'm sorry," she mouthed before she closed the door. Betty would have gone on the cruise with them. In a few months she would be looking for another job. Tom should have apologized to *her*.

<What did she say? Don't pretend it was nothing. I saw you shake your head at the open door.>

He filled a plate with almonds, a buttered roll, and some cheese. "Long day at work is all. I'd hoped to not have to work while I was with you." Tom entered her room.

The wires and plugs were a shock every time. People said he would get used to it, but he never did. They snaked around her body and through the simple gray smock she wore. A machine arched over the head of her bed. The machine panel was littered with switches and ports. Each light was color-coded to its port and body part, and blinked inside a hair-thin wire. The bed moved to bring her body to an upright position. Her arms and legs had been propped up on several pillows. Her head rolled to the side, falling forward. The bed stopped.

<Could you please…>

Tom reached forward and adjusted her head. Her eyes blinked slowly and heavily. Not because she was tired—she slept for several shifts during the day and night. When she was tired she usually fell into sleep easily and quickly. He envied her for that. She'd always been able to turn off her mind efficiently, even before her symptoms showed.

He situated a pillow and blanket to keep her head in a more comfortable position, trying not to touch her more than necessary. In the early stages she had lamented over her loss of touch, relying on others to help her with simple movements. Anita insisted Tom's touch was always welcome, but he didn't want to assume. Although he always managed some excuse to linger. He slid his fingers over her jaw, pretending to help her gently coax her mouth shut, so she wouldn't drool. After several tries she swallowed with effort. Her wavy black hair, wet from her bath, had been pulled into a bun.

<Why do you have to cut the Barker Testament? It's the most interesting piece.> The speakers in her room were more clear, just as Betty had said. The computer did an excellent job of capturing the innocent, curious lilt in her voice.

"It's because of the Peace Talks on Jupiter. They're afraid if there are some religious references that it will be in bad taste. Considering…"

<Of course. But did you read it? Did you see the file I sent you?>

"I…" He checked the data on his tablet. He *did* have a file from her. "No, I just noticed it."

<So Barker was a missionary sent to Kaus four or five hundred years ago. A lot of the supporting files are just now reaching Earth. His early reports were instantly controversial. He claimed he found stories that were so similar to the Bible on other worlds. It was as if history were repeating itself. I've found so much more since then. Why is this not huge news?>

"I don't know—"

<And there's even video. It's like a whole other world has been opened up. You've got to include this! If it's true, it changes things.>

"Oh?" Tom sat on the edge of the bed, considering the debate her ideas opened up. The wars that had been fought over beliefs—not just in this solar system, but across the universe. Anita knew the history. What harm could it do to let her imagine and wonder? And for once she didn't want to talk about what guests to invite to the funeral, what flowers to order, or who would give the eulogy.

"Tell me about them." His hand slid easily into hers. Her fingers fluttered at his touch, but she didn't have enough strength to hold his hand. "I can't include them. I just can't, but how about you and I make this our own special project?"

She was silent for a moment. Her eyes were open with excitement—a rare sight.

<I would love that! In fact, this is exactly what I've been looking for.>

Maybe he didn't need a cruise to give Anita an experience before she deteriorated. Before she ended.

※

The bacon sizzled. Tom flipped his eggs and scanned through his project edits. He had the rough idea and was working on the finer details of the project while Anita slept.

<Smells amazing. Better than my breakfast of...what is this again...liquid slop?> Her tone was light and joking, but guilt hit Tom all the same.

"I'm sorry, I—" He turned the fan on, opened a window. He hadn't thought Anita would be awake. She'd been quiet for the last hour.

<Please don't be. Maybe it is a bad reminder.>

Tom stared at his breakfast, looking at it differently. He should have had cereal. Lately reminding Anita of the things she couldn't have anymore had added to her reasons to disconnect.

<Oh, come on now! You can't change things. Sometimes I wish I'd let go early on and not have to suffer though this. I mean, we went on a few dates ten years ago. I didn't really stop to think about the consequences of our relationship. I didn't think about what it would put you through. I feel selfish.>

"Selfish? It's more selfish to push me away. I would have thought I had some flaw. I wouldn't have known what happened to you." Tom knew that if there was no Anita in his life he'd have been alone. He wasn't the type to have lightening strike twice. When he first saw Anita he loved her. He'd never imagined anyone else filling that spot in his heart. Finding out that Anita felt the same seemed like a mathematical improbability.

<Listen to us. We're a sad pair. How is your project coming along?>

"Almost done." Tom scraped the bacon and eggs onto his plate and carried it over to a table. He brought his tablet and pulled his focus back onto his project, tapping and zooming to get the frames he needed. "If I finish this afternoon we'll have some time together before I have to leave. I feel like I've pulled off a miracle. Mr. Filmore better give me a promotion for all this effort."

<You should ask for one.>

Tom laughed. "No. That was a joke. He would never do such a thing. He doesn't even know me. He thought I was an intern."

<Then *make* him notice. You've done so much for Silver Arch. When I pull news articles and media I see your work being praised. Don't let yourself fade into the background. You're special.>

"You only think that because it's me."

<Maybe. Maybe I'm biased. I don't think so.>

Tom harrumphed, smiling around his bite of eggs.

<I've pulled together some of the best Testament stories. Maybe you could look them over later? I posted a few up for discussion on my fan site. I don't have many followers, but so far it's caused an interesting debate.>

Tom had become fascinated about the Barker Testament as well. Anita had uncovered more stories overnight. Along with the Jesus story she'd found evidence that matched the stories in the Koran, the Old Testament, even some of the Bhagavad Gita.

<*Imagine,*> she had said. <*Heaven exists. Imagine this is not the end.*>

He knew she'd meant her end. Somehow this story had given her something writing a memoir could not. Although Tom didn't find it as interesting, or even as profound. He still thought it seemed too coincidental. Too much reading into things that were probably not there. Seeing patterns where none might have existed before. But crushing Anita's hope didn't sit well with him and so he played along.

"It's comforting to know that we could meet again. Maybe in another life?" He had choked on the words, swallowing several times to get them out.

<*Do you think this proves the existence of a universal creator or disproves it? I can see arguments for either side.*> She had mused

through the night as she searched the archive library. <*The stories repeat themselves. Proof that we are not unique in our world; we didn't have anything special with our prophets or great men. In fact, as a universe we are cruel to those who are great. It's depressing.*>

"But we have happy stories to balance it out. Just as there are happy stories on other planets."

<*Always the optimist.*>

"You've been a bad influence."

Tom finished his breakfast, the memories of the night floating through his mind. "I'm excited to see what you've worked up."

"I can't wait to show you," she said, in a tone that indicated she had a pressing question to follow. "I was wondering, thinking actually. If I'm doing well now, what's the rush? I mean I could postpone the arrangements a week or two—until I've got some bigger signs of further neuro degradation."

Tom's chest expanded, as though he was able to breathe for the first time in a while, but he also didn't want to cling to the possibility only to have his hopes dashed. "I only need another hour on this and then the rest of the day is yours."

<Absolutely. I'll leave you to it.> She was silent for a minute. Then: <That's odd.>

"What is it?" Tom rinsed his plate and dried his hands in a hurry. He calculated the last time he'd given her meds. "Are you okay? Do you have some pain? I could get the—"

<No. It's not that. I think your project has taken up some of the bandwidth. The system is just a bit slow. Or my site is down?>

Tom frowned. "I haven't been downloading or uploading this morning. We should give the repair company a call. See what's happening."

<No. It's fine. I'll run a diagnostic while I nap.>

Then there was silence. Anita didn't wake until dinner.

⁂

Back at the office, Tom unloaded his bag and dusted out his coffee cup and set it on his claimed seat (in the coveted corner). He placed the completed file chip on his desk. He would wait for Mr. Filmore so he could turn it in directly. Then he'd request a raise and time off. Starting now. He stretched, set his feet up on his table. Instead of waiting in the coffee line, he watched the group from where he sat. He'd go up when it was less crowded.

Bianca walked by his area, carrying several hangers of dry cleaning.

Tom flagged her down. "Did you have any problems with your internet this weekend?"

"Yeah, it was a slow Sunday morning, but it came back up right away. Got to love the service the north side of the city gets, right?"

Tom nodded in agreement. "Right." Bianca continued to her desk, placing her hangers in the dry clean rack. Anita's internet was still down this morning. Odd.

⁂

Tom didn't get an appointment with Mr. Filmore until after lunch. But he had spent every moment until then preparing his speech. He'd gathered statistics, performance reviews. Anita had sent him positive messages and encouragement.

<*Good luck,*> she had said. <*I'm going to take a short nap. I hope to wake up to happy news!*>

How is your internet? Should I call repair?

<*It's fine now. It's dropped off a few times, but comes right back. My fan page had some damage, but I fixed it. Nothing to worry about. Just focus on that promotion.*>

And when he strolled into Mr. Filmore's office he was ready. Yes, he strolled—he didn't know he *could* stroll—most of the time he shuffled. Tom tapped his data bracelet and the images, charts, graphs appeared before them.

"Top ten edited pieces of the century. The Newman Award. The most talked about films of our generation. They all have something in common. Me."

Tom delivered the line with confidence. Mr. Filmore glanced up from his screen. Tom stood a little straighter.

"I'm not just here to deliver to you a project. One that was impossible, I might add—and I did it in a weekend, but I'm also here to ask for a promotion."

Once he got that, he'd negotiate his vacation and explain his circumstances. He'd mention Anita. He knew she didn't want people to feel sorry for her, but he couldn't *not* tell his boss if he was asking for two months off and a raise. He'd pull the pity card if he had to. He was doing it for Anita. He was doing it for both of them.

"But first the Hwain Documentary. You'll see that it's all there, exactly to your specifications."

Mr. Filmore's eyebrows furrowed. He stared at the file. He played the opening scenes and watched as if he were judging a pageant and none of the contestants meet his standards.

Tom didn't let the less-than-positive reaction deter him. "If you'll just look at this graph I've put together, you'll see that I—"

"We can't use this. The Hwain documentary has been cut."

Tom's smile fell. "What? But you wanted it by Monday. I worked on it all weekend."

"I'm sorry, Tim—"

"It's Tom."

"—This came from higher up. You'll find that a lot of shows get cancelled. When you're no longer an intern—"

"I'm not an intern. I've been an employee of Silver Arch Entertainment for thirty years. I know you've only been here for five, but people here know I'm the one who gets things done. I got *this* done. I did everything you asked. It's ready to go. I changed the tone and the focus. It's mostly about Kaus and geographical similarities with other surrounding planets—"

"It's done." Mr. Filmore stood and tugged his jacket. "The documentary has been canceled. I can see you've worked hard on it, and I'll keep that in mind. Now if you'll excuse me, I have a meeting to get to."

Mr. Filmore dropped the edited file and the original into the delete bin.

※

Tom sat at his table for an hour after the meeting, staring straight ahead. His co-workers whizzed by on their way to the editing table, which was situated in the middle of the office floor today. The whispers started after they passed his desk. "Will he be sacked?" They had wondered. "Will he finally quit?"

Tom breathed deeply. Might as well get it over with: *Bad news.*

He didn't type anything more. Anita didn't answer. She knew what it meant. Thankfully, she knew to leave him alone. Tom didn't need another witness to his failure.

※

"Tom, it's Betty."

Tom shifted the phone from one ear to the other, resituating his bag. The other passengers swayed as the train shimmied on the tracks.

"Betty. Hello. Everything all right?" Several passengers cleared their throats and scooted in their seats, turning away from him. Tom lowered his voice. "I should be there in an hour."

"…she's frantic…Do you have a copy?"

"I'm sorry you're breaking up. I think it's the tunnel."

"It's all lost…when you get here…" And then the call dropped.

Tom gripped his phone, waiting for his stop. It was the longest hour of his life.

※

<When the net came back up, the research, the notes, they were gone,> she told him.

"We backed up your memoirs." Tom sighed in relief when he got to the apartment. He'd imagined all sorts of horrors before he got there. "I'll check." He scanned the external hard drive. "See, right here. But you should have access through your computer."

<I can't. I don't know what's wrong. But I don't see them. Everything is missing.>

"We'll get repair in here. We'll figure it out. Must be a glitch in your software."

<It's like I had all this freedom and now I have nothing. What if this is it? What if—>

"No, it's not." Tom's heart skipped a beat. He was glad Anita couldn't monitor his vitals. Or read his body language. Those systems were down. "You're still able to communicate. No use dreaming up disasters. It's a software glitch, nothing else."

<Make a copy. Make one now. I don't care about the memoir. Get all the Testament research. I think that's what they were after.>

"What *who* was after?"

She didn't elaborate.

He pulled the files. Several were difficult. He checked them. Corrupted. "I've got most of them," he lied and ran a virus and malware scan. "Just making sure I have them all."

She didn't respond. Heat crept up his neck and into his cheeks. He should tell her, let her know. They were her projects. He opened his mouth, shut it. He formed the words in his mind, how to frame it positively. If she realized it was gone would she push the date up? Would she see it as some sign to check out early?

<I'm tired. Will you set the files aside? I'm going to rest.> She sounded defeated. Her words came slow and difficult.

"It will be here when you wake up. We can go over your notes."

<I'd like that.> She sounded hopeful.

Or maybe that was wishful thinking.

She slept through the night. She'd never done that before. Tom would wake every hour or so, expecting her to call with some need or reassurance. But none came.

In the morning she couldn't form complete thoughts. Her voice software caught every other word.

He called repair.

※

He didn't go to work. Anita faded in and out for most of the day. When she was lucid she'd ask about the Testament stories.

<Please tell me again. Please read it back to me.>

Repair was working on the problem. Her software had somehow absorbed the glitch from when the net went down, it caused several of her systems to fail, which in turn accelerated the deterioration of her medical state. Her doctors called. The news wasn't good.

"Should we?" Tom's voice cut out, almost like he couldn't physically say the words. He didn't want to offer it to her as an option. But if she was in pain… "Do you want to move the date up?"

She wouldn't respond. Or she couldn't.

<Tell me the stories again. The Testament stories.>

That was her only request.

※

That night Tom gathered all the information from the repair crew, going over each item. The doctors consulted with him over Anita's situation. The damage was irreversible. Her system was dependent on the computers, and when they went down, her symptoms worsened. The nerves and neuropathways weakened to the next stage. Her communication skills had suffered and the computers could only substitute for so much. There would forever be a gap until she passed away.

It was exactly what Anita had feared would happen, and why she had considered voluntary disassociation—the medical term for unplugging from the computer that gave her the ability to communicate and move. She wanted it to be within her control and go on her own terms.

Tom scanned the list from repair.

Possible targeted computer virus.

They'd tracked an attack on her personal page. It was not designed to cause system failure, but it looked as though Anita had tried to patch the problem herself and it had involved some of her higher-level software.

Tom saw the flurry of activity on her discussion about the Barker Testament.

He closed the report.

On Wednesday Tom made a quick trip to Silver Arch to drop off his projects. There was a note from Mr. Filmore to see him in his office.

He went straight there. If he was going to get fired, he wanted to know right away. Then he could go back and be with Anita.

He approached the office. The door was open but two people from advertising were there. The three ignored him until he knocked on the open door. They poked their heads up.

Tom held out his note.

"Oh, right, Tom, I saw you were sick yesterday. I hope you're feeling better."

Tom stepped back, unsure of what to think of his boss both remembering his name and also noticing he was missing.

"I'm fine, sir. It was a personal day. A—" he never knew how to refer to Anita. Girlfriend? Live-in partner? "A friend was very ill. It doesn't look good. I'll be out the rest of the week."

"Of course." Mr. Filmore motioned for the other two in the room to give them privacy. They walked past Tom with a nod; one patted him on the shoulder. The door clicked shut.

Tom reached for the door. His hand hovered over the handle. The tension in the room shifted. His skin seemed to shrink over his bones. "Am I fired?"

Mr. Filmore reared back. "No. No, absolutely not. I think I've overlooked you, and I hope to make it up to you."

Tom froze, his eyes widened, his mouth hung open. He closed it.

"When you get back we can talk about that raise."

Mr. Filmore looked him in the eye and didn't look away. It was the same assessing gaze a lion might give a gazelle. The room's temperature seemed to drop. Tom shook.

"I just wanted to let you know that our stockholders have approved a digital re-organization. You'll notice some of your files for past projects have already been deleted off your workstation. Just to tidy things up."

Tom kept his gaze on Mr. Filmore, unable to respond. He wanted to ask him about the Barker Testament. He wanted to know why he'd been assigned the project, only to have it canceled. Why did Anita get attacked the same day? If someone didn't want the information out for whatever reason, why didn't they just ask? Or was it all just a coincidence? Was he paranoid? Was he really that unlucky?

Tom squeezed his fists, clenched his jaw.

Mr. Filmore's face flickered into concern. "Take all the time you need."

Tom packaged up the Testament files, dropping the disk into an envelope. He set it on the counter.

It was his imagination, right? Anita wasn't targeted because of the stories? If she could find them, anyone could.

He shook his head and ran his palms down his face. He needed more sleep. More time to decide.

"I think it's time to start thinking about quality of life," Dr. Rashamond's voice was quiet on the phone. She'd gone over all of Tom's questions. There was no way Anita could gain back what she'd lost.

"What if someone targeted her?" Tom flattened his hand on the envelope. He needed an excuse to send it. To have someone find out why someone would want this information kept from the public. "What if this wasn't an innocent accident?"

"It will be very hard to prove, but my recommendation is to get a lawyer to answer those questions you might have."

A lawyer would recommend an investigation. It would cost time and money Anita didn't have.

"We can schedule her to be removed from the computers next week. I'm sorry, but her results indicate that she may only last a few days after that. I'm going to send you information on alternative care services that specialize in this sort of thing and also contacts to help with…arrangements."

"I was thinking of taking her somewhere. A cruise—"

"That might be difficult at this stage. Maybe before, but…" Dr. Rashamond sighed. "I'm sorry. She may also be past the stage where she is aware what is going on around her."

Tom waited a beat, almost expecting Anita to disagree. Nothing came.

Tom closed his eyes and thanked the doctor for her time.

He didn't know if Anita was targeted in the wrong place with the wrong information, but he did know a guy who would find out. One of the most hated investigative reporters alive, but he knew how to find the truth, no matter how ugly it could be. He'd want to explore the Barker Testament himself, assess its validity. At the very least it would continue Anita's research. It would be her legacy and last wish.

He sent an email.

⁂

"What is this?" Betty hung her coat on the hook inside Anita's room.

Tom arranged the blue silky fabric to flow across Anita's window. The holographic images of the ocean flashed on the walls.

"It's a cruise," Tom replied simply.

Betty turned in a circle. Tom watched from the corner of his eye to see her run her hand along the twinkling lights that draped from the ceiling under loops of iridescent fabric.

"Does it look like the stars in the sky?" he asked.

Betty smiled. "It looks lovely." She patted Anita's hand. "You're well taken care of. This cruise is going to be exactly what you've always wanted." Her voice wobbled. Maybe because Betty knew that it wasn't perfect. It wasn't the cruise they'd meant it to be, but it was all they had.

"Tell a story," Anita's voice repeated. The only thing she would say now.

"I'm going to tell a story, Anita." Tom assured her. "I'm going to tell your story to as many people as possible." He thought about the email. He'd not gotten a response yet, but he knew his guy would come through. It was too much to pass up. Hidden histories around the galaxy. Conspiracy. "But first I'll start with just one."

Betty moved from her position where she leaned on the bed. "How about we order the food? There is a great seafood place that delivers."

Tom was about to answer when Anita said, "Shrimp." He would have thought he imagined it, but she said it again.

Betty and Tom froze.

Tom reached for Anita's hand. "We will have plenty of shrimp. Don't worry."

Betty clapped her hands over her mouth and waved away tears. "Well, then, I better get to it. Shrimp it is!"

"Yeah," Tom said, a faint smile on his lips. "Shrimp. You always wanted me to have the best."

Betty scurried out of the room.

Tom had spent the morning on the phone with another entertainment industry. A possible lead on a better job and an exclusive on Anita's story.

"Tell a story." Anita said when Betty was gone. "Tell my story."

Tom clutched the envelope in his pocket. "Don't worry. We will."

Book Three

Cross Purposes

MIKE RESNICK

1

Gar Matthews stopped reading his hate mail and looked up from his elegant desk at the man who was awkwardly approaching him.

"Yeah?"

"Mr. Mathews?"

He nodded but made no reply.

"My name is Tom Inkle," said the man uncomfortably. "I believe you're expecting me?"

Matthews frowned. "I am?"

"I sent you a pair of messages."

"Well, that explains it," said Matthews with a shrug. "Do you know how many messages I get in a week?"

"I have no idea."

"Lots." A smile flashed briefly across his face. "Some of them don't even threaten me with bodily harm." A pause. "What was yours about?"

"A long-lost or long-misplaced file concerning the discoveries and conclusions of one Joshua Barker."

Matthews shook his head. "I'm sorry, Mr. Inkle, but I—" Suddenly he blinked very rapidly. "Wait a minute! This was the report by the nut case who thinks they crucified another Messiah on another planet?"

"He doesn't seem to have been deranged," replied Inkle. He indicated the envelope that was tucked under his left arm. "I have the document with me, and of course I can also load it onto your computer or any other device." He shifted his weight uncomfortably. "I am probably breaking half a dozen rules by showing it to you."

"Then why bother?"

"You seemed the most likely to be able to do something with it."

"Do *what*?" asked Matthews. "Show that God had a Messiah on more than one world, or that you don't have to be human to be a barbarian and nail up a decent member of your race?" Matthew learned forward. "Jesus came along, and the Jews got thrown out of Jerusalem for two millennia. He died for our sins, but the sinning didn't stop. You know how many major military operations have included genocide since they nailed him to the cross? So what exactly do you propose that I do with this revelation that some other race uses nails too?"

Inkle shrugged helplessly. "Prove it. Disprove it. I'm sorry if I seem a little vague. I've been having some personal problems, and I've been under a lot of pressure. Anyway, I want you to figure out if it was misfiled, or if the government has kept it buried all these centuries for a reason – and if so, find out what that reason was."

"Why not just ask your superiors?"

"If it was buried on purpose, then it'll be their job to keep it buried."

Matthews looked amused. "And see to it that you're buried too?"

"It's possible," answered Inkle seriously. "At the very least my employment would be terminated, and if it was hidden for a reason, they might terminate my very existence." He paused uncomfortably. "It's not much of a life, but I have someone who depends on me."

"You have a lot of confidence in your government," said Matthews with a smile. "The odds are ten-to-one they'd fuck it up, or kill the wrong man."

"Perhaps," agreed Inkle. "And perhaps not. But *you*...no one would dare lay a finger on you!"

Matthews chuckled at that. "You know how many death threats I get every month?"

Inkle looked genuinely surprised. "You do?"

"Freedom of speech has always sounded like something immutable and engraved in stone, but so has freedom to threaten speakers. Or in my case, writers."

"I just figured that *The Iconoclast* appears on so many planets that—"

"It just means I get threats in more than five hundred languages," replied Matthews with a smile. "Those weren't secretaries or research assistants you passed in the outer office, Mr. Inkle. They were bodyguards."

"Four of them," mused Inkle aloud. "Must cost you a fortune."

"It would if I paid for them. Fortunately the publishing syndicate picks up the tab."

Inkle frowned. "Now I'm wondering if I should even have contacted you. I mean, if anything gets you threats, it'll be the Barker Report. Prove he was right and half the people in the galaxy—and not just the humans—will want to kill you. Prove he's wrong and the other half will." He stared at Matthews. "But either way, you'll sell an extra billion copies of your column."

"If I agree to take a few months out of my life fiddling with this silliness," responded Matthews.

"If you do," agreed Inkle. "I just figured you had the most clout of anyone I might be able to interest in it. And for whatever reason, it's going to take someone with considerable clout to follow it up. If *The Iconoclast* appeared daily, or even weekly, I wouldn't have bothered; but it only comes out when you've got the goods on something, and by this time, everyone knows that when it shows up, whether it's about the scandal that brought down the government on Isda IV or the disaster that destroyed those mining asteroids in the Bareimus belt, or anything else, you've *got* the goods."

"I appreciate your confidence," said Matthews. "Here's my offer, and it's non-negotiable. I'll study the file, and if I think it's worth the effort, I'll take the job on. I will fund any research out of my own pocket, and I will keep any and all revenues that the story generates. Once you walk out of this office we don't know each other, and if the government demands that I turn over your name to them, I will go to jail before doing so."

"That's your standard business agreement?" asked Inkle, surprised.

"That's right," said Matthews, extending his hand. "Now we sign it in blood."

Inkle frowned. "I beg your pardon?"

Matthews smiled. "We shake hands. No signatures, no writing, no DNA or fingerprints."

Inkle extended his hand, and Matthews took it.

"You know," said Inkle, placing his envelope on the desk, "I've been reading you for years."

"I'm properly appreciative," said Matthews in bored tones.

"I guess everyone tells you that."

"Well, the ones who don't tell me that explain how they're going to dismember me."

"I guess that concludes our business," said Inkle, and Matthews nodded an affirmative. "May I buy you dinner before I leave?"

Matthews shook his head. "We don't know each other from this moment forward." He reached into his desk and pulled out a small receipt, handing it his visitor.

"What's this?"

"Ticket stub for your orchestra seat. The hottest musical extravaganza in the system." Another smile. "Why else would you have come here?"

"So you *did* expect me!"

"No. I buy a seat every night, just in case we need to prove why some visitor had a reason to be here other than meeting with me."

"No wonder you've stayed in business for so many years," said Inkle admiringly.

"Close to twenty," replied Matthews.

"Twenty-two," Inkle corrected him. "I researched you before I came. But the government computers are a little unclear about your name."

"It's always been Matthews."

"I mean your first name."

"It's Edgar," replied Matthews. "Everyone else shortens it to Ed, so I decided to use Gar just to be different. Besides, I've already got a common first name, but it's tacked on at the back: Matthew."

Inkle chuckled. "I guess you've been an iconoclast from the start." He patted the envelope where it sat on the desk. "I think you'll find this worth the effort. I wouldn't have brought it otherwise."

He turned and walked out of the office.

Matthews poured himself a small glass of Denebian brandy, tossed the envelope in a drawer, and began reading the report, labeled *Kaus 12TC7*, on his computer. By the time he was done he knew he'd found his next column.

2

He didn't believe in wasting time, so just before sunrise the next morning Gar Matthews boarded his ship and took off for Kaus. He spend most of the day re-reading the report, and using his computer to find out what had happened to both Joshua Barker and to the planet itself.

What he learned was somewhat less than instructive. The Reverend Joshua Barker had spent the rest of his life—all seven years of it—on Kaus, after serving his initial ten years as a missionary. He never wrote a follow-up report, never wrote a book, never built a church. Was he dismayed by what he'd written about in his report? Was he afraid to preach his own religion until he learned how true a rival religion might be? Or had he just given up on both societies, human and Kaus? There was no way to tell.

Studying the past few hundred years of Kaus's history wasn't any more helpful. They'd had some wars, but managed not to annihilate any sub-species of the race. They'd discovered a cure for *ropagi*, their most serious and widespread disease—but people still died of it, just as Men still died of cancer and other diseases that had been "cured" for millennia. They had erected some churches to their "savior," but there were at least as many devoted to other religions, just as Jews, Muslims, Hindus, and others outnumbered early Christians back on Earth.

"Computer," said Matthews, "did Barker ever marry?"

"Not while in the human community," responded the machine. "I can find no record of a marriage on Kaus, but it is entirely possible that marriages go by another name, or are not registered at all, on that world."

"Damn!" muttered Matthews. "I was hoping he might have some descendants living on the world. Still," he added with a shrug, "what the hell could they tell me four hundred years later?"

"I can find no record of any Barker living on Kaus," announced the computer.

"Surnames can change over the generations," replied Matthews. "See what you can find, but don't use all your brainpower on it. See if there are any Christian churches on Kaus."

"No churches," said the computer half a minute later. "And I am unable to find any descendants of Joshua Barker using any surname."

"Oh, well, it was a thought. I assume we have an embassy there?"

"A small one: one ambassador, with a staff of three."

"Well, at least I'll have someone to talk to." Suddenly Matthews frowned. "What the hell does he need three assistants for? As far as I know we don't have any commerce with Kaus."

"Correction," said the computer. "The ambassador is a *she*."

"Well now, that's interesting," remarked Matthews. "I'd ask you what she looks like, but you'd probably describe her muscular and vascular systems in disgusting detail. So let's get back to the assistants."

"Working…" The machine fell silent for twenty seconds. "One is a security guard, and the other two are low-level diplomats who accepted the posting in the hope—or so one may surmise—of more important future postings."

"And of course our taxes are paying for that," said Matthews sardonically. "Okay, Cuddles. That's all for now."

"Who is Cuddles?"

"You are."

"I do not have a name," said the computer.

"Now you do," said Matthews. "It helps humanize you."

"I do not want to be humanized. I am content to be a computer."

"Fine," replied Matthews. "Now you can learn to live with adversity."

"But—"

"Stop whining and tell me far we are from Kaus."

"In millimeters or inches?" responded the computer.

Matthews grinned. "Damn it, Cuddles—I'm starting to develop a real fondness for you. Tell me in hours and minutes."

"Eleven hours, seven minutes, twenty-three seconds—and my name is not Cuddles."

"Actually, as near as I can tell, your name is Ship, or maybe Hey You," replied Matthews. "Okay. Make me some dinner, run the holos that Barker sent back of Kaus on the viewscreen again, and have the chair massage my back."

"Yes, Gar."

"Then, after I digest my dinner, I think I'll go to sleep. You don't need my help to pilot this thing."

"No, I don't."

"Did I detect a note of petulance?" said Matthews.

"No, Gar, you did not."

Matthews leaned back and enjoyed the massage while staring, for the fifth time that day, at Barker's holos.

"Hell, it even *looks* hot," he remarked.

"Current temperature is thirty-five and one-half degrees Celsius," said the ship.

Matthews did the math in his head rather than ask the ship. "Damn, that's ninety-seven degrees Fahrenheit! No wonder it looks hot."

"The section of the planet you see is in early spring."

"There damned well better be a story here, that's all I've got to say," muttered Matthews.

He was soon asleep, woke up feeling unrefreshed, went to the galley, and poured himself a cup of coffee.

"Terrible stuff!" he muttered.

"I also have tea, water, milk, carbonated fruit drinks in three flavors, beer, wine, whiskey, vermouth—"

"Enough," growled Matthews. "*Everything* is terrible when you first wake up."

"I wouldn't know," replied the ship. "I never sleep."

Matthews wandered over to a viewscreen. "Where the hell are we now?"

"About two hours from landing on Kaus. I have contacted them, received permission to land, and have been given the proper coordinates. I did not know if you will be contacting the embassy immediately, so I left that decision up to you."

"You trust me to decide, do you?"

"That is a joke, is it not?" said the ship, following its question with a monotone "Ha, ha."

Matthews wanted to glare at the ship's brain, or its mouth, but he didn't know where either of them were. Finally he sat down in the ill-named pilot's chair. "Contact the embassy."

"Yes, Gar."

"And tell me who I'll be talking to."

"Edward Messina."

Matthews frowned. "I thought you said the ambassador was a woman."

"She is."

"Named Edward?

"He is her assistant," responded the ship. "You must go through him to get to her."

"Okay, put him on."

"One moment."

The ship went silent, and then the holographic image of a middle-aged man appeared.

"Yes?" he said.

"Good morning," said Matthews.

"Evening," the man corrected him.

"Whatever. My name is Gar Matthews. I sent you a couple of messages."

The man smiled. "Ah, yes, Mr. Matthews. We've been expecting you. My name is Edward Messina."

"Pleased to meet you," said Matthews. "I'm told we'll be landing in a couple of hours. I'd like to meet with the ambassador."

"She's at dinner now," replied Messina. "I can contact her and tell her to come back to the office…unless this can wait until tomorrow?"

"What time does she come in?"

"In the mornings?" said Messina. "800 hours, embassy time."

"Embassy time?" repeated Matthews, frowning.

Messina chuckled. "You wouldn't believe the local clocks. Unless you enjoy a fifty-seven hour day."

"800 hours it is," said Matthews.

"See you then."

"By the way, what's her name?"

"The Ambassador?" replied Messina. "Zabeth Winstock."

"Zabeth?" repeated Matthews, frowning. He turned to the computer. "Not Eliza or Liz or Beth? That's a hell of a way to shorten Elizabeth."

"There are" – the ship paused briefly – "nine thousand, three hundred and seventeen Zabeths living on human-populated worlds. There are only one hundred seventy-four Gars."

"Whatever would I do without you?" asked Matthews sardonically.

"Die of asphyxiation, freeze, and float across the void for all eternity," replied the ship.

"Choices, choices," muttered Matthews.

3

"Not much light," said Matthews as he looked out at the spaceport. "Does it get any brighter later in the day?"

"No," said the ship.

"You got anything positive to say?"

"I made a perfect landing."

"I can't tell you how thrilled I am." Matthews stood on the doorway. "I'll leave my gear here and come back to sleep at nights."

"Understood."

"Unless someone offers me better accommodations, which shouldn't be difficult." He looked at an approaching vehicle. "This must be my ride."

He walked down a ramp that the ship lowered for him and stood on the ground, hands on hips, waiting for the vehicle.

"Mr. Matthews?" said a mechanical voice.

"Don't tell me," muttered Matthews. "I'm talking to a robot."

"In a manner of speaking," came the reply. "I am KT-12, your personal conveyance for the duration of your stay on Kaus."

"You got a female voice you can use?"

"Yes," answered KT-12 in melodic tones.

"Good. From this point on I'll be calling you Katie."

"Whatever you desire."

"I can't tell you how happy it makes me when anyone called Katie tells me that," said Matthews, climbing into the vehicle. "Now take me to the Ambassador."

"Roger," replied KT-12.

"No, Zabeth."

"I mean—"

"Never mind."

They drove across the dull, featureless landscape for about five minutes, at which point the vehicle turned to its right and approached a long, low building, stopping at the main entrance.

"We have arrived," announced KT-12.

"I would never have guessed," remarked Matthews, getting up and walking to the door, which slid open. "Wait here."

"For how long?"

"Until I come out."

"I am blocking traffic."

"I don't see any traffic," said Matthews. "I'd be surprised if this joint gets three visitors a month. But what the hell, go park fifty feet away if it'll make you happy, Katie."

"Yes, Gar."

"That's yes *sir* to you."

"Yes, Sir Gar."

Matthews grimaced. "Never mind," he said, stepping down to the cracked pavement and walking to the embassy's entrance.

"Name?" said another mechanical voice.

"Gar Matthews."

"You are expected. Please enter and take the first corridor to your left."

Matthews did as he was told, and found himself in a corridor lined with a dozen doors.

"Last door on your right," said the voice.

Matthews did as he was told, opened the door, and entered what was clearly an outer office. A pudgy man in his early thirties stood up and extended a hand. "Mr. Matthews?" he said. "I'm Edward Messina. Pleased to meet you."

"Ditto," said Matthews.

"I mean it," continued Messina with a smile. "You're our first visitor in more than a month."

"I can believe it," replied Matthews. "This isn't exactly a tourist destination."

Messina chuckled. "I'd call that an understatement."

"Is the Ambassador in?"

"Yes. I told her you were coming to see her this morning. "He walked to a door along the back wall, opened it, and gestured Matthews to follow him into a larger, more elegantly-appointed office, the walls covered with plaques and holos of commendations. Seated behind a desk made of some alien hardwood that was from neither Earth nor Kaus was a slender woman Matthews estimated to be in her early forties.

"Mr. Matthews?" she said without getting up.

"Yes," he replied. "And you're Ambassador Winstock."

"Let's be informal, shall we?" she said. "I'm Zabeth and you're Gar."

"Whatever makes you happy," said Matthews. He indicated a chair that faced her desk. "May I sit down?"

"Of course." She turned to Messina. "You can leave us, Edward. I'm sure I shall be quite safe with Gar."

"You're ruining my reputation," said Matthews with a smile as Messina left the office and closed the door behind him.

"And quite a reputation it is," she said. "I thought your name sounded familiar when Edward told me you were coming, so I had my computer do a little research. I'm thrilled to be sitting here with the Iconoclast himself."

"The author of *The Iconoclast*," he corrected her.

"Same thing," she replied. "Your reputation precedes you, Gar." She paused and stared at him. "Is that short for Garfield?"

He smiled. "Not quite."

She shrugged. "Makes no difference. Now, what can I do for you?"

"I'm here because of the Barker Testament."

"The Barker Testament?" she repeated, frowning.

He nodded. "Right."

"I've never heard of it."

"Oh, shit!" growled Matthews. "Of course you haven't! I wasn't thinking. The damned thing's been lost or hidden for centuries!"

She stared at him curiously. "I'd comment," she said at last, "but I have no idea what I'd be commenting *about*. Perhaps you'd care to enlighten me."

"I'm sorry," said Matthews. "You ever hear of a man named Joshua Barker?" He paused. "The Reverend Joshua Barker?"

"No," she replied. "Should I have?"

He shook his head. "No, I suppose not." He stared at her for a long moment. "What about a Kausling named Click?"

Zabeth frowned. "Click? No, I'm afraid not." Then suddenly her demeanor changed and she leaned forward. "Just a minute!" she said excitedly. "Do you mean Kleek?"

"I don't know," said Matthews. "Do I?"

"What can you tell me about this Click you're looking for?" she asked.

"Not much," he admitted.

"You've never met him?"

"He's been dead for centuries."

"By God, I'll bet it's Kleek!" she exclaimed. "I repeat: what can you tell me about Click?"

Matthews spent the next fifteen minutes summarizing the Barker Testament. "I think someone in the government believed in all its implications," he concluded. "Why else call it the Barker Testament rather than the Barker Report?"

"And it's been misfiled all these centuries?"

He nodded. "Purposely or otherwise."

"Can you offer any suggestions as to why?"

"Could be that some atheist was afraid people would read it and think God was creating Messiahs all the hell over the galaxy," he replied. "Or it could be that someone took pity on Kaus and didn't want a few hundred missionaries coming here to explain why *our* Messiah was the true one. Or it could be that an exceptionally devout file clerk felt his Christianity was threatened by Barker's story and made up his mind to hide it." He paused. "Or it could just have been misfiled. Happens hundreds of times a day, maybe thousands."

"How very interesting," said Zabeth, leaning forward, and Matthews could tell by her demeanor that, if anything, that was an understatement.

"Well?" he said after a moment.

"I'm sorry," she said, brushing a wisp of graying hair back from her forehead. "I'm still taking it all in. Everything fits!"

"Could you explain that, please?"

"I know very little about Joshua Barker, but I'll be willing to bet I can guess to within ten years when he was on Kaus. You see, there *is* a religion here. Just one. No hints of Judaism or Islam or the others that you say Barker thought he saw. And the religion isn't Christianity, not as anyone knows it. But as you know from Barker's account, a number of people – not an especially large number, I would guess – worshipped the Kausling who was crucified, and felt he was something very special."

"Are you going to tell me that Kleek is the way the Kauslings pronounce 'Click'?"

She nodded with certainty. "There was never an organized religion as such until about four centuries ago, when a Kausling named Kleek codified a bible of sorts – primarily a verbal one. It describes the Venerated One's last days, his crucifixion, and then sets forth a series of rules, laws, behaviors, call them what you will. Since the one who was crucified was the ultimate authority for them, and since I can think of no more accurate term for Kleek than the first high priest, or the equivalent of the Pope, I feel you'd have to call it a religion that, whether true or not, was founded on a crucifixion."

Each fell silent for a moment as they considered what they had learned.

Finally she smiled at him. "So, Mr. Matthews, do you think your trip was worth the expense and the effort?"

He nodded his head. "I'll need a few days to convince, not myself, but my readers. I'll have to dig up enough facts and get enough interviews for them – but it looks like the pure quill:

a real religion, started because of a crucifixion." He paused. "I wonder if it's as phony as Christianity."

"What makes you think Christianity is phony?" she asked quickly.

"What makes you think it isn't?" he replied with a smile.

"It brings people comfort."

"So do morphine, and heroin, and alphanella seeds."

"It has its share of authenticated miracles."

"Authenticated with video, or camera, or sketch artist, or cave paintings, or unreliable eyewitnesses?" responded Matthews.

"Mr. Matthews, this interview is over," she said suddenly.

"Oh?"

"I happen to be a Christian, and I find your comments offensive. I should have expected them from the Iconoclast, but…"

"I meant no offense," he assured her.

"You make your living by challenging people's beliefs and offending them. I understand that. You don't want to prove that Kleek's religion might be true, but rather that both his and mine are false, and I have no intention of helping you do so. I will instruct Edward to guide you wherever you wish to go, or provide you with a native guide if you prefer, and should you run into any difficulties with the local populace we are your embassy and will do what we can on your behalf. And now, if you will pardon me, I have work to do."

Matthews got to his feet, turned, and walked back into the outer office.

Damn! he thought. *Maybe this column is getting to me. I use to have to try to offend people. Now I seem unable to avoid it.*

4

"So," began Messina as he led Matthews to KT-12, "where am I taking you?"

"I'm trying to remember what it's called," replied Matthews, frowning and concentrating. "Ah, yes – the Steam Field."

Suddenly Messina smiled. "Okay, now I know why she's mad at you. She's a very devout Christian, our ambassador."

"She doesn't mind *you* going there, I notice," remarked Matthews.

"I'm not Mr. Iconoclast, with a readership of, what, ninety million?"

"A hundred and thirty million," Matthews corrected him automatically.

"And they won't miss your column while you're digging around on Kaus?"

"If I wrote about things that only took a day to research, I'd have a hundred and thirty readers, not a hundred and thirty million."

"Makes sense, I suppose," said Messina without much interest. He uttered a low command and the doors opened. "Okay, hop in."

"How far are we?"

"From the Steam Field? Maybe a couple of hours."

"Will we be passing any cities along the way?

Messina chuckled. "This is Kaus. There aren't any cities."

"They're all rural?"

"They're all primitive."

"Still?"

Messina frowned. "Still?" he repeated.

"I thought maybe things would have changed since...well, since..."

"Since the crucifixion?" suggested Messina.

"Yeah."

Messina shook his head. "They hadn't changed by the time Kleek showed up, and as far as I can tell they haven't changed all that much since then. He codified some of their beliefs, but since they already held those beliefs..." His voice trailed off, and he shrugged.

The vehicle left the vicinity of the embassy and headed off across a rough, fog-enshrouded plain.

"Oof!" grunted Messina as they hit an unseen bump. He uttered a pair of coded commands, and suddenly the vehicle was skimming along two feet above the surface.

"Not much to see," commented Matthews.

"You're going to have a hard time believing it," said Messina with a smile, "but this is probably the garden spot of the planet."

"Probably?" repeated Matthews.

"I haven't been here long enough to see the whole thing, knock wood," said Messina with a chuckle. "This is not the most coveted of all assignments, Mr. Matthews."

"Gar."

"Gar," repeated Messina. "And I'm Ed."

"So what are you doing here, Ed?" asked Matthews.

Messina grinned. "My number came up in the draft. Not that we have a draft, but with worlds like Kaus it's three years and out. I was waiting for reassignment when my predecessor's time was up."

"Ambassadors usually serve more than three years on a world," noted Matthews.

"Ambassadors, maybe; their staffs, rarely. Not on worlds like Kaus, anyway," said Messina. "I don't even know why we're here, except to stop anyone else from claiming it. No minerals worth mining, no fissionable materials, not much of anything."

"My experience has been that we're on most of the worlds we're on just so someone else won't be there spreading *their* influence and culture when we want to spread ours," said Matthews.

"*You* try to spread our culture here and see where it gets you," laughed Messina.

Matthews looked out at the seemingly empty world. "I see your point."

"By the way, Gar, I noticed that the boss was mad at you. You want me to put in a good word with her when we get back?"

"Thanks, Ed, but I've learned to live with making people uncomfortable."

Messina nodded his head. "She's pretty devout."

"What makes you think that has anything to do with it?" asked Matthews.

"There's only one thing that makes this world even mildly interesting, or minimally less boring," responded Messina, "and that's that some local got himself crucified for creating a new religion."

Matthews shook his head. "Not quite."

"I beg your pardon."

"As near as I can understand it, he didn't get crucified for creating a new religion," said Matthews. He smiled. "As near as I can tell, a new religion came into being *because* he was crucified."

"Big difference," said Messina with a shrug.

"Big enough," answered Matthews. "The Romans crucified a lot of men. Only one crucifixion started a new religion."

A smile spread across Messina's face. "I see your point. And the boss must have seen it too. That's why she's annoyed with you."

"Surely I'm not the only guy in the last four centuries who wanted to see the spot where it took place."

"True," said Messina. "But you're the first iconoclast. That's what iconoclasts do, isn't it – attack accepted beliefs, that is?"

"From time to time," said Matthews.

"But of course," continued Messina, "you're not here to attack the Kauslings' beliefs. I mean, hell, you've yet to see your first one. They're never going to leave the planet and preach Kleek's morality anywhere else." He paused, and then suddenly grinned. "I've got it! No Man is going to believe in the Kauslings' religion. If you can prove it's identical to Christianity, even the way they both began, and one is invalid, then..." He concluded with a laugh.

"Don't understand me so fast," replied Matthews. "First I have to see if there *are* any similarities."

"You know there are. Kleek's guy got himself nailed to a cross, or the equivalent of one."

"So did a ton of Jews and more than a few Romans," noted Matthews. "Now, did the religion exist in some form *before* Barker got here, or did he somehow inspire Kleek to start a religion based on Barker's?"

"Who the hell is Barker?"

Matthew spent the next half hour condensing the Barker Testament.

"Well, I'll be damned!" said Messina when he was done.

"Only if Kleek and the Gospels are right, Ed," answered Matthews with a smile. "Hell, I don't even know if Kleek's religion postulates an afterlife or has a definition of sin. That's what I'm here for." He looked out across the barren landscape. "Damned lucky that's *all* that I'm here for. You sure this planet is still populated?"

"Not heavily, but yeah, it's populated. We'll be coming to a village in another few minutes."

"It's amazing."

Messina frowned. "What is, Gar?"

"That Barker or anyone else of his era would even consider traveling here."

"Why not? I mean, hell, we already had FTL travel back then."

"Yeah, but if you flew here in a direct line at light speeds from Barker's world, everyone there – everyone you ever knew – would have died of old age by the time you got here, thanks to the time dilation effect. It's only the past three centuries that we started mapping and traversing the galaxy's millions of wormholes and traveling in what I'd call Real Time." He looked at the bleak landscape. "Maybe a preacher with a calling, someone like Barker, would leave it all behind to spread the Word if he believed deeply enough – but you gotta wonder about the crew that took him. I mean, they sure as hell couldn't have been leaving any husbands or wives or kids behind."

"On the other hand, if they left a few thousand credits behind in their bank accounts, they might be millionaires when they returned," said Messina with a smile.

"Or they might return to a bunch of rocks where their world used to be."

"My friend the iconoclast," chuckled Messina. "At least the wormholes are good for you. Couldn't go abroad in search of material if your worshipping audience was dead and buried by the time you filed your story."

"Certainly couldn't have that," agreed Matthews. He frowned. "Am I imagining it, or are we actually slowing down?"

"Village coming up in about twenty seconds," replied Messina, looking at a readout on the vehicle's screen. "Brace yourself, Gar. We're not talking megalopolis here."

Matthews peered ahead through the haze, and finally a cluster of some thirty mud huts came into view.

"They've got a spaceport and they live like *this*?" said Matthews.

"It's *our* spaceport, not theirs," answered Messina. "We built it, we use it. They're about two steps out of the stone age."

"I'm surprised they've got a bible."

"Well, it's not a bible the way you and I might define it, Gar," said Messina.

"Okay, what *is* it?"

"An oral tradition, repeated by rote, word for word."

The vehicle came to a stop. A pair of Kauslings who were walking nearby barely glanced at it. No one emerged from the huts to greet it.

"They must be used to seeing you," commented Matthews.

"I get to this village four or five times a year," replied Messina.

"And that's all the excitement and hospitality they show?"

"They've known about us for quite a long time, Gar. We've had a presence on the planet for four centuries. We have nothing they want, and I must say that until you came along they had nothing we wanted."

Matthews frowned.

"Yeah, I know," continued Messina. "Why have a presence here at all?" He half-smiled, half-grimaced. "Just to stop the Kroll Empire or the Jaskin Confederacy from laying claim to it. It serves no useful purpose for us, but it's a little close to some of our major planets for someone else to set up shop here."

Matthews nodded. "Probably as good a reason as any our government has come up with. Well, let's go be obnoxious tourists."

"Right," said Messina. "Open!"

The doors opened on his command, and they stepped out onto the uneven rocky ground.

"I'd love a breeze," remarked Matthews. "Except it would probably blow so much dust I'd have to go back inside the vehicle." He surveyed his surroundings and shook his head. "How can anyone live here?"

Messina sighed deeply. "This is where they chose to build their huts, Gar. For all we know it's the most desirable real estate in the hemisphere, and Kauslings would kill to live here."

Matthews chuckled grimly. "And you say *I'm* an iconoclast."

"Well, let's proceed," continued Messina, heading to the clustered huts, and Matthews fell into step behind him.

A female Kausling emerged from a hut and faced them.

"What do you want?" she asked in broken Terran.

"This is a visitor from another world," said Messina, gesturing toward Matthews. "He would like to ask you some questions about Kaus."

She looked at Matthews with no change of expression. "As you wish," she said.

The breeze became stronger, whipping up some dust.

"May we enter your hut, where we will not be bothered by the weather?" asked Messina.

"*I* am not bothered by it," she said as she turned and entered it.

Matthews ducked his head and followed her, with Messina right behind him. He looked around, saw three objects that might be furniture but nothing shaped for him to sit on, so he sat down cross-legged on the dirt-covered stone floor. Messina elected to remain standing, his back to the doorway.

"My name is Gar," said Matthews, extending a hand.

The Kausling stared at it, making no move to take it.

"This is a gesture of friendship among members of my race," he continued.

"Ah!" said the Kausling, stretching her hand out in front of her but making no attempt to touch Matthews'.

"I would like to know about Kleek," said Matthews, lowering his hand.

"He lived many years ago," answered the Kausling.

"Is he the one who found the cross?"

"Cross?"

"The structure upon which the great being was nailed."

"He knew of it," she replied, "but he did not find it. It was known before."

"And do you know the name of the being who had been crucified?"

"Crucified?"

"Attached to the cross."

"He who was of the steam," replied the Kausling, as if clarifying. "The great one."

Matthews nodded. "Yes, the great one. Had he a name?"

"I am sure he did," she answered. "But it is lost in the swirling mists of Time."

"So you know nothing of him?"

"I know he speaks to us through Kleek."

"He does?"

The Kausling nodded. "Among other things, he tells us to tolerate you."

"How very kind of him," said Matthews, certain that the note of sarcasm would be undiscernible to her alien ears.

"Kindness was his essence. We try to live as he did." She stared expressionlessly at him. "Have you any other questions about him?"

"Just one."

"Ask," said the Kausling.

"He was kind, you say," began Matthews. "He has taught you kindness, and gentleness, and tolerance."

"True. And your question?"

"Why was he killed?"

The Kausling stared at him without answering.

Ten minutes later, when he turned to leave her hut, she was still staring silently at him.

"You might have gotten the same kind of response from Saint Peter," remarked Messina as they walked through the village. "Who knows why someone would kill a being who is demonstrably chosen by your god, or is perhaps a god himself?"

"That doesn't fly," said Matthews. "Whether Jesus was a son of God or not, even *I* know why the Romans killed him."

After he interviewed four more Kauslings and received the same response from each, he turned to Messina.

"They don't seem hostile, Ed," he said. "Is it just that they're ignorant, or won't they discuss their faith with an outsider?"

"I don't know," answered Messina honestly. "I've never tried to discuss it with them."

"Well, clearly I'm not going to get any answers here," said Matthews, heading toward the vehicle. "It's time to go to the one place where I might find some."

"Oh?"

Matthews nodded. "Take me to the cross."

5

It was another ninety minutes before the vehicle began slowing down.

"Getting close?" asked Matthews.

Messina shrugged. "I think so."

Matthews frowned. "You *think* so?"

"I've only been here once before, Gar," was Messina's answer. "I know we're close. We'll find it."

"Only once?"

"How often to you think the Roman ambassador's non-religious underlings went out to see Golgotha?"

"Point taken," acknowledged Matthews.

"Based on my previous experience, we'll run into their equivalent of the priesthood when we get there," explained Messina. "They won't object to our presence, as long as we comport ourselves in a properly respectful manner." He grinned suddenly. "And I've been trained to do *that*."

"Based on the Barker Testament, no one seemed to pay much attention to the cross or the Steam Fields by the time he'd arrived," commented Matthews.

"Figures," answered Messina. "Based on what you told me, the religion began with Kleek, who was a contemporary of Barker's."

"But Click, or Kleek, wasn't the only one who knew that the damned thing was their equivalent of a cross, or that their holy man – well, holy Kausling – had been nailed up there."

"How many Jews do you suppose walked right past Golgotha before the Bible was codified?" shot back Messina. "Or even after, given the literacy rate back then?"

Matthews shrugged. "I've got to stop equating this religion with Christianity. From what little I know of it, Jesus was pretty much revered – not by the Romans, of course – as a teacher, maybe even a prophet. No one even seems to know the Kausling's name, just that he was, according to Click, a great and moral member of his race."

"Steam's heavier off to the left," noted Messina. "Let's head over that way."

"Do you remember heavy steam from your first trip?"

"I think so. Truth to tell, I wasn't paying that much attention. To the best of my memory I was dictating some report."

"The Ambassador took you here?"

"No, a woman named Callahan. Worked in the office. She was transferred to Ballitora IV a year ago." He shook his head. "Lucky girl. Whole damned planet's a hunting concession. You wouldn't believe the size of some of the beasts they've got there."

"Let's concentrate on hunting for the cross," said Matthews.

"I'm working on it," answered Messina. "I seem to think it was either in some gorge or just next to it."

"How many people on Kaus?" asked Matthews.

"People?"

"Kauslings."

Messina shrugged. "Maybe five million."

"How many believe in the religion?"

"Beats me," came the answer. "Personally, I haven't met any who don't. Or at least, who don't know about it. They just don't seem anxious to talk about it with humans. They don't seem interested in talking about anything, now that I come to think about it."

"What do they do with their dead?"

Messina shrugged again. "I've no idea. Bury 'em or burn 'em or eat 'em or throw 'em into the gorges. I've never seen a graveyard. Come to think of it, I've never even seen a dead Kausling body."

"I suppose if there was some religious ceremony, you or some member of the staff would know about it."

"Theoretically," answered Messina. "But you have to understand, Gar – we only have a staff of four, including the Ambassador."

"Four?" repeated Matthews, surprised.

"There are close to eighty thousand inhabited or colonized worlds, and this little dirtball's only got five million beings on it. That's pretty much par for the course

Matthews was silent for a long moment, peering out through the window. "Why the hell would anyone want to live here?" he muttered at last.

"On the planet?" asked Messina. "They were born here."

"No, I mean right here, in the middle of all this steam. It can't smell too good, it's blinding, there are gorges to fall into all the hell over, and unless you eat rocks you have to go afield every time you want a meal."

Messina had no answer, so he kept silent. Then, a moment later, he leaned forward. "Damn, I think we're here!"

"Doesn't look a hell of a lot different than the last dozen clumps of huts we passed," remarked Matthews.

"These are new."

Matthews stared at them and frowned. *"New?"*

"Well, new*er*," answered Messina. "Less than four centuries old."

"How can you tell?"

"They found something better than mud to hold them together, and they figured out that they need ventilation toward the roofs." He paused. "Well, toward the tops."

"Where I come from, they'd have been torn down three and a half centuries ago," said Matthews. "Probably longer."

"Where you come from, they probably have tools and a variety of building materials," replied Messina with a smile.

"Well, let's get out and look around. You know anyone here, Ed?"

"No," answered Messina. "I've only been here once, on the orientation tour a couple of years ago. But they don't have a tourist industry. My guess is that even though I won't know any of *them*, they'll remember *me*."

"Good," said Matthews. "Maybe I can get some answers. At the very least, they won't shoot us for intruding." He shrugged. "Hell, maybe they're happy to have visitors."

Messina seemed genuinely puzzles. "Why?"

"Maybe they've got a few centuries of pent-up evangelism waiting to burst out."

Messina chuckled. "Let's see if you can get them to talk about it at all."

"Did you try?" asked Matthews. "When you were here, I mean?"

"Of course not. I didn't even know they *had* a religion until we pulled up here and my guide told me about it." Messina fell silent for a moment. "Oh!" he said suddenly. "I just remembered. If you see a Kausling wearing any kind of hat or headgear at all, he's a member of the priesthood – or what passes for it."

"They got a priesthood?" replied Matthews. "I haven't seen any sign of it. No robes, no one wears little crosses, I'd be surprised as hell if a world like this had a printing plant let alone a bible."

"I'm just telling you what I was told."

"Okay, let's get out of this contraption and walk around. I want to see the cross."

"It's not *exactly* a cross, not the way I'm sure you're envisioning it."

"Don't be that sure," said Matthews with a smile. "I do my homework. I've read Barker's Testament."

"Then you probably know a hell of a lot more about the religion than I do, Gar," admitted Messina.

"You've been here long enough to learn about it."

Messina shrugged. "I'm just a wage earner. It's not as if I've been assigned to the Vatican. I'll be out of here in another year, and no one will know or care." He paused. "No wars. No scientific breathroughs. No medical breakthroughs." A sudden grin. "I think maybe the only way you *can* have an effect on this world is to get crucified."

"No, thanks," said Matthews, returning the grin. "I could dictate and work my computer verbally while I was nailed up there, but how could I scratch where it itched?"

"A telling point," laughed Messina, ordering the door to slide open.

The two men stepped out into the muggy, humid air and looked around.

"This way, I'm pretty sure," said Messina, heading off to a deep, steam-filled gorge.

Matthews fell into step behind him, and after they'd walked perhaps eighty yards they found themselves facing a Kausling wearing an elaborate five-pointed hat, far and away the most sophisticated thing Matthews had seen since landing.

"Your purpose?" said the Kausling.

"My companion does not speak your language," said Messina in broken Kausian. "I shall act as interpreter."

"That will not be necessary," replied the Kausling in equally broken Terran. It turned and faced Matthews. "Your purpose?"

Let's see what he does with an answer he's not expecting, thought Matthews. Aloud he said: "To lead a moral life, honor my friends and family, and never raise a hand in anger."

The Kausling stared at him silently for almost a full moment, then finally spoke.

"You are welcome," it said. "My name is Kblix."

"My name is Gar. I am pleased to meet you."

"Why have you come to this holiest of places?" asked Kblix.

"To learn about he who was crucified."

"I do not know the word."

"He who came before the others, and who died here."

"Ah!" said Kblix. "You wish to see where he died."

"Yes," answered Matthews. "And to learn about him, about what he has taught you and those who have followed him."

"You are a wise being, Gar," said Kblix, turning and starting to walk to the gorge. "Come."

They walked through the Steam Fields for a few minutes, and then they came to it. It didn't look like a cross, not the kind Matthews had seen on every Christian structure and Bible, not the kind people wore around their necks…but then, it wasn't created to hold someone shaped like a man.

He stepped a little closer, frowning. "What is *that?*" he asked, pointing.

"The Holy One's arm," answered Kblix. "Or what is left of it."

"And you've left it there all these centuries?"

"He has no need of it, and it shows us that of all the similar structures, *this* is the one where he died."

Seems a little crude, but not unreasonable, thought Matthews. *How the hell do* we *know that Golgotha is actually where Jesus was crucified?*

"And you abide by his teachings?" asked Matthews aloud.

"Yes."

"Have you a bible?"

"I am not familiar with the term," said Kblix.

"Something where his beliefs and teachings are codified, so that they will never be forgotten or misinterpreted."

Kblix shook his head – a very human gesture, thought Matthews. "He led by example, not by lecture."

"May I ask what some of the tenets of your religion are?"

"I do not know that word."

"Tenets?"

"Religion," responded Kblix.

"You're kidding!" exclaimed Matthews.

"That is another word I do not know."

Messina laid a hand on Matthews' shoulder. "I don't think he's kidding, Gar."

"Okay," said Matthews with a sign. "Kblix, a religion is a set of beliefs and moral principles that you live by. For example, if you think it is wrong to kill your neighbor, that is a religious principle, a tenet of your religion, and you try to obey it."

"Ah!" said Kblix. "I think I understand. We do not lie, because *he* thought lying was wrong."

"A sin, right."

"A sin?"

"Something that's wrong," replied Matthews lamely. "Now I have another question, and I mean no offense by it. I am simply trying to learn about your...beliefs."

"Then you may ask."

"You live by his principles," said Matthews, indicating the petrified arm.

"True."

"But you do not have a written language. You have no books. You have no video. You have no computers." He paused to see if the Kausling was going to ask what any of the words meant. When Kblix remained silent, he continued: "So how do you know what he said, what he believed?"

"Kleek has told us."

"But Kleek himself has been dead for centuries."

"Those he spoke to spoke to others," said Kblix.

"How can you know that they spoke accurately?"

"Accurately?"

"How do you know that what they said was exactly what Kleek had said to them?"

"Why would they lie?" asked Kblix.

"I don't mean that they lied," said Matthews. "But how do you know they didn't misremember?"

"They heard it," answered the Kausling. "They repeated it."

"There is a party game..." began Matthews.

"Party?"

"A game," amended Matthews. "Ten people sit in a circle. The first one whispers a secret to the second, the second whispers it to the third, and so on, all the way around the circle. Then the tenth and last person repeats what he heard, and they compare it with what the first person said – and is it never quite the same."

"That is foolish," replied Kblix. "You should not permit liars to associate with each other, or the truth could be lost forever."

"You know what a book is?" asked Matthews. "And writing?"

Kblix inclined his head, which Matthews assumed was his form of nodding it. "Yes."

"We codify our Holy One's teachings a book we call the Bible, so that no one can ever forget it, or state it incorrectly."

"That is a very good idea," began Kblix.

"Then–?

"If you distrust your memory, or if your leaders are liars," concluded Kblix.

Matthews decided that all he would do was offend the Kausling if he continued on this subject, so he asked to be shown around.

"But you have seen where the Holy One died, where what is left of him remains," answered Kblix.

"Is there anything left of Kleek?" asked Matthews. "Not Kleek himself, of course. He has been dead for centuries. But anything to show he was here, that he became the interpreter of your truths, that he was a revered teacher?"

"He is down there," replied Kblix, pointing to the deepest section of the gorge. "If there is anything left of him."

"Has no one ever attempted to find out?"

"Why?" asked the Kausling. "He is dead."

"Did he live near here?" asked Matthews. "I know he met and spent some time with Joshua Barker, a member of my race."

"He never mentioned Joshua Barker."

Matthews resisted the urge to say, "*How do you know?*" and instead asked if Kleek had gone from village to village spreading the Word, or if pilgrims had come to the Steam Fields.

"He traveled as long as he was able," answered Kblix, "and then after age and injury had taken their toll, people came here to listen to him."

"And what he said is what your people have lived by ever since?"

"Most of us. Some never believed in the precepts, some believe but lack the strength of character to follow the teachings of Kleek, based upon the life and values of the Holy One."

"But there's no question in your mind that the teachings are true?" persisted Matthews.

"None."

"Have you ever asked the Ambassador or any of her predecessors to take you to other worlds so you can share your beliefs with them?"

"Our truths are for ourselves," responded Kblix. "Why speak to Men or Shemrees, whose only Holy Ones were killed in similar ways, and have derived their truths from them?"

"Shemrees?" said Matthews sharply.

"Inhabitants of Beta Piscium II," interjected Messina. "They call themselves Shemrees – or at least the Kauslings call them that."

"Are you saying," says Matthews to Kblix, "that the Shemrees preach a religion based on one of them being crucified?"

"Crucified?" asked the Kausling, frowning.

"Nailed to a structure not totally different from the one you showed me."

"Ah," said Kblix. "Yes."

"How do you know this?" persisted Matthews.

"We have been visited by the Shemrees."

Matthews gave Messina a questioning look.

"Not to my knowledge," responded Messina, shaking his head.

"It was many generations ago," said Kblix. "They tried to teach us their truths, but we had our own. They killed many of us, but we would not relinquish our own truths for theirs. And one day they realized this and went away."

"And of course, since no one writes or codifies history, this is all hearsay," said Matthews.

"Hearsay?" repeated Kblix. "I do not know this word either."

Matthews shrugged. "It's okay." He scanned his surroundings one last time. "We're done here. I want to thank you for your time and your help, Kblix."

"I wish you peace and contentment," replied the Kausling.

"I wish you the same." Matthews turned to Messina. "Okay, Ed, I'm ready to go."

Messina led the way back to the vehicle, and a moment later they were skimming along, eighteen inches above the surface.

"Where to now?"

"To my ship."

"Let me guess," said Messina with a smile. "You're going to Beta Piscium II."

Matthews nodded. "There's no story here. A primitive race that's illiterate, that passes on not only its religion but its history solely by word of mouth. No one saw their Holy One get crucified. I mean, yeah, that's probably his arm on the cross, but so what?" Suddenly a smile of anticipation crossed his face. "If it was only Kaus, I'd call it a fluke. But if the creator of still another religion was nailed up on Beta Piscium II, I'd call it a *pattern*."

"I hadn't looked at it that way."

"I have a feeling I may be onto something *big*, Ed – something that may be worth more than one column."

"Just be careful, Gar," replied Messina.

"Careful?"

Messina nodded. "Earth, Kaus, Beta Piscium, they seem to have one thing in common," he noted. "None of them seem to have any compunction about killing moral beings."

"Then I'm off the hook," said Matthews with a smile. "Moral beings are another union."

Three hours later the vehicle pulled up to Matthews' ship, and less than five minutes later it had taken off for the Beta Piscium system.

"Hey, Cuddles!" said Matthews as they passed through the stratosphere.

"That is not my name," replied the ship.

"Answer to it anyway. How long should it take to get there?"

"I will reach the McGruder Wormhole in six minutes. After one hundred seventy-three minutes I will transfer to the Beronitis Wormhole, and—"

"I don't want the route, just the ETA," said Matthews.

"Two days, seven hours, and twenty-one minutes," responded the ship.

"Good," said Matthews. "That should certainly give you enough time."

"For what?"

"Finding worlds that practice a religion that originated with the crucifixion of a figure that is now deemed holy."

"Man has colonized or populated seven thousand three hundred and—"

"No," interrupted Matthews. "Christianity counts as one religion, no matter how many worlds it's on, no matter how often it's been perverted or misinterpreted. I need to know how many *other* religions came about through similar circumstances." He paused. "I'll give you a hint. Kaus is one of them."

The computer was silent for perhaps twenty seconds. "There is nothing in any of my databases to confirm that."

"I know," said Matthews. "Now check Beta Piscium II."

This time the silence lasted only six seconds. "There is such a religion there."

"I know," said Matthews. "Okay, Sherlock. I'm gonna take a nap. Let me know what you've found when I wake up."

"Sherlock is not my name either."

"You prefer Cuddles?"

The ship was about to answer, but Matthews was snoring gently before it had the opportunity to do so.

6

Matthews woke up, stretched his arms, and yawned.

"You are awake," said the ship.

"You must have been the brightest one in your class," muttered Matthews. He got slowly to his feet, made his way to the lavatory, and emerged a few minutes later.

"Well," he said, sitting down again. "What have you got for me?"

"Greenbriar," responded the ship.

"Greenbriar to you, too," said Matthews. "What about it?"

"There is a religion there that seems to have originated when a very popular member of the dominant species was affixed to a structure."

"Be a little more specific. *You* are a structure. And I could affix something to you with nails, tape, glue…"

"I cannot describe it as a crucifixion," responded the ship, "because the physical structure of the being is such that a cross could not accommodate it."

"But they nailed him to *something*," persisted Matthews.

"Yes. If you will turn your attention to the screen on your left, I will reproduce the device, which is now considered the most meaningful symbol of the religion."

Matthews looked at the screen, which displayed something resembling a hoop with five boards hung across it at identical intervals.

"What the hell was he, a tennis ball with ten legs?" he muttered, frowning.

"He was a member of the race known as Ralti."

"So was he a Ralt, a Ralti, or a Raltling?"

"He was a Raltor," answered the ship. "A male of that species."

"Figures," growled Matthews. "Where the hell is the Greenbriar system? I never heard of it."

"It is in my database as the Wiskinti system."

"Then why the hell aren't you calling it Wiskinti II or III or whatever?"

"Because it was named Greenbriar by the human who mapped it," replied the ship.

Matthews frowned. "Not the Raltor, but the human cartographer?"

"The Ralti are – or at least *were* – a very primitive race with little or no interest in geography."

"That doesn't make any sense," complained Matthews. "I don't care how primitive they are, if a religion is going to spread across a world, they *have* to know where it's spreading."

"Of course they do," agreed the ship.

"Well?"

"They are limited teleporters."

"Limited?" asked Matthews. "What do you mean?"

"They cannot teleport off the planet."

"So by the time a Raltor is fifteen years old, he's probably seen every site worth seeing on the whole damned world," concluded Matthews. "Okay, no sense mapping it or establishing trade routes if you can just wish yourself from here to there. Have they got any other tricks up their sleeves?"

"They do not wear sleeves," responded the ship, "but they are also partial telepaths."

"Partial?" repeated Matthews. "How does one be a *partial* telepath?"

"They can identify and physically – or geographically, if you prefer – pinpoint the source of thoughts, but they cannot read them."

Matthews stared at what he assumed was the very center of the ship's mechanical brain. "Why do I have this urge to ask if you've been drinking?"

"Because these concepts are beyond your experience," replied the ship.

"Shut up."

The ship immediately fell silent.

Matthews considered what he had heard for a few minutes, then spoke again: "Did you find any other crucified religious figures?"

"Yes."

"Many?"

"That is difficult to say. Many of these are either very new or very minor religions, just beginning or on underpopulated worlds, and in some cases it is very difficult to distinguish truth from myth."

"How the hell hard can it be?" demanded Matthews.

"Most religions begin in primitive societies," responded the ship. "Very few spacefaring or even industrial societies create religions, though some accept or adapt existing ones."

"Some religions are pretty well-documented," said Matthews.

"Almost none."

"Hell, Christianity is," said Matthews. "We know the day Jesus was born. We know the day he died. We not only know how he died, but where he died. I'd call that well-documented."

"There are many errors and inconsistencies in his story," said the ship.

"Bullshit."

"His family went into Egypt when he was a boy to avoid one of Herod's bloodlettings," said the ship. "Is that correct?"

"You know it is."

"What I know," replied the ship, "is that there is no historical record of *any* bloodletting during Herod's reign."

"Okay," admitted Matthews. "Maybe his childhood isn't as well- documented as people think, but his adulthood was."

"And his crucifixion has been accurately told and re-told during the past three millennia?"

"Yes," replied Matthews. "Maybe I don't believe in the religion, but I do believe that Jesus was crucified exactly the way it's been reported in the Gospels ever since they were written."

"And the sign above him, at the top of the cross, was 'King of the Jews'?" continued the ship.

"Yes. It was in Greek or Aramaic or some other language, and as I recall it read *INRI.*"

"What if you were to learn that it read INBI?"

"INBI?" repeated Matthews, frowning.

"That's a translation of the Greek letters," said the ship. "It means the same thing: King of the Jews."

"Big deal."

"How about INBK?"

"Same thing," said Matthews.

"Not quite."

"Oh?"

"It means King of the World. That implies a totally different religious concept, does it not?"

"Are you saying that they hung INBK over his head?" demanded Matthews. "How the hell would you know?"

"I don't," answered the ship. "But the Gospels were not codified in print for many years, and it is very likely that none of the apostles had the gift of literacy. Therefore, they may have remembered the inscription incorrectly, since they were trying to remember the shape of letters with which they were unfamiliar."

"Bullshit," said Matthews. "Your job is to do what I tell you and bring me legitimate data, not idle speculation. Now, what about the other worlds?"

"I will display a list for you," replied the ship. "I cannot attest to the veracity of all the details, only that on each world a religion now exists that had its origin in the crucifixion-like death of its founder or prime member."

"And none of these worlds were maybe visited by Christian missionaries *before* their religions came into being?"

"Not that I could ascertain. Certainly no more than two or three."

"Out of how many?"

"Seventeen thus far. I am continuing my research even as we speak."

"Seventeen?" said Matthews. "That seems like a lot."

"There are hundreds of thousands of worlds in the galaxy," replied the ship. "It is actually very few."

"I don't think you know how unique Christianity is."

"Now that I have begun my search, I must agree with you."

"Agree with me about what?"

"That I do not know how unique Christianity is," said the ship.

Matthews got up, walked to the galley, pulled out a bottle of whiskey, realized that he had just awakened, shrugged, and took a long swig anyway. Then he returned to the chair he'd been occupying.

"Look," he said irritably, "nothing sells like religion, except for sex, and there's nothing sexy about being nailed to a cross. This could be one of the biggest, most lucrative stories I've ever covered, and I don't want your negativism fucking things up."

"I am only following your orders."

"I didn't order you to argue with me about what the hell it said on Jesus's cross!" yelled Matthews.

"Yes, Gar."

"Yes, Gar, you'll do what I tell you and nothing else, or yes, Gar, I *did* tell you to argue with me?"

"I am a logical mechanical entity, incapable of argument," replied the ship.

"I bet you believe that."

"I *know* that."

"Same damned thing."

"Not so," said the ship. "I am a machine, and therefore incapable of a belief system."

"So if some entity the size of a planet suddenly appeared in space just ahead of you, raised his hand, and said 'I am the Lord and I command you to stop!' you wouldn't do so?"

"I would stop," answered the ship. "I must protect my own existence whenever possible. But the fact that I would stop to avoid a collision, or harm to my passengers – which in this case would be you – does not mean that I would have any empirical reason think he was the Lord."

"And if he performed a miracle?"

"I would be compelled to find a logical and scientific justification for the effect."

"I said miracle, not effect," said Matthews.

"I am not programmed to believe in miracles."

Matthews glared at the ship's control panel. "You know, Cuddles, I am starting to develop a real dislike for uppity spaceships."

"Is 'uppity' in some way related to 'up'?" asked the ship.

"Forget it."

"Done."

Matthews sighed deeply. "How long before we reach the Berta Piscium system?"

"Forty-six hours and twenty-nine minutes."

"Okay," said Matthews. "Keep looking through your data banks. I'm gonna grab some breakfast."

"Yes."

"Oh...and one more qualification: the ones who were crucified have to have been involved in the inception of some religion, or at least a cult. I mean, the Romans probably crucified a few thousand Jews. Only one mattered to future generations."

"Understood."

Suddenly Matthews tensed, then stood stock-still for a moment.

"Damn!" he exclaimed.

"Is something wrong?" asked the ship.

"No," said Matthews. "But I have another chore for you. How long before you've finished hunting up crucifixions?"

"I do not know," replied the ship. "Probably between ten and twelve hours. But I can multi-task, if you wish to assign me another chore."

"Yeah, I do. As you pointed out, crucifixion was a common death penalty back in Israel three millennia ago – and as you also noted, the Holy One was the only Kausling to be crucified."

"The only one that we know about," qualified the ship.

"The only one that we know about," agreed Matthews. "Do you see what I'm getting at?"

"No, I do not."

"After you've found all the worlds where a crucifixion led to a new religion or belief system, I want you to closely examine the ones where crucifixion was, if not commonplace, at least not unknown – and see if you can determine why only one victim became worshipped and none of the others did." Matthews allowed himself the luxury of a smile. "I have a feeling that this may be an even bigger story than I thought."

"In what way?" asked the ship.

"Are you challenging me again?" asked Matthews irritably.

"No. I simply have a compulsion to learn."

"All right," said Matthews. "If the ones whose deaths were instrumental in creating religions all said or did something in common, all expressed the same philosophy, all did something that seemed mystical on the surface of it, then we'll know *why* beings of every race have believed in some mystical being or power greater than themselves when there is absolutely no empirical proof of it."

"I will do so, Gar."

"And do it objectively," concluded Matthews with a chuckle. "I don't want *you* getting religion."

7

"I need a decision, Gar," announced the ship.

"What's the problem?"

"There are four spaceports, plus an orbiting hangar. Where shall I ask permission to land or dock?"

"Four *and* a hangar?" repeated Matthews. "I have a feeling we're not in Kansas anymore, Toto."

"I have never been in Kansas, and my name is not Toto," replied the ship.

"Don't take it personally," said Matthews. "We all have our shortcomings."

"I still need a decision."

"Let me think," said Matthews. "Who do I want, a priest or an historian?"

"None of the spaceports is attached to a church or a university," said the ship.

Matthews was silent for a few seconds, then shrugged. "What the hell," he said. "It doesn't matter. I don't want a religious or an historical education. I just want to find out about the guy they crucified."

"I don't think 'guy' is an appropriate terms, Gar."

"It'll do for the moment," replied Matthews. "Okay, which of the four is closest to a metropolis?"

"They are *all* close to major cities, Gar," said the ship. "Why would anyone choose to land in the mountains or the desert or—"

"It's not a matter of where the ship chooses to land," interrupted Matthews, "but where the powers-that-be don't want it to crash if anything goes wrong – and don't start quoting me statistics on how few ships have crashed in the last fifty or hundred years."

"Yes, Gar."

"Okay, so they're all near major cities. Connect me with one."

"Working...proceed."

The holograph of a uniformed alien appeared before Matthews. It was bipedal, covered with tan fur, it wore a single garment that covered most of its torso and legs, it had some emblems attached to the garment at chest level, and it was clearly standing next to a number of machines.

"How may I help you?" it asked, and it was obvious that its voice was being filtered through a translating mechanism.

"Greetings," said Matthews. "My name is Gar Matthews, and I would like permission to land."

"May I ask the purpose of your visit?"

"Research. I'm a writer."

"You are a troublemaker," said the alien.

"I beg your pardon?"

"Your column is not unknown to us. That is why it does not appear anywhere in the Beta Piscium system."

"May I land or not?" demanded Matthews.

"For how long?"

"If I can find someone to talk to me, no more than two planetary days," responded Matthews. "If I have to do the research myself, longer, since I do not speak or read you language, nor am I familiar with your planet. In fact, I had never heard of it until a few days ago."

"Who do you wish to talk to?"

"An historian, or a member of your church."

"We have many churches."

"Of your major religion, then."

"Are you here to discredit our religion?" asked the alien.

"No. I just need to have some questions answered that are quite peripheral to an article I'm writing. Once I get my answers I'll be on my way and neither you, your planet, nor your religion will ever hear of me again."

"I doubt that," said the alien. "All right, Mr. Matthews, you may land. You will be given a guide, and the moment you ask any questions concerning our defense or our politics, you will be summarily returned to the spaceport and told to leave the system. Is that understood?"

"Perfectly," said Matthews.

"I have just transmitted landing coordinates to your ship. With any luck, this is the last time I shall speak with you."

The image vanished.

"I love you too," muttered Matthews.

"I have the coordinates, Gar," said the ship. "I should touch down in about twenty-eight minutes."

"No sooner?"

"There is a lot of traffic."

"Yeah, I guess there must be." Matthews was silent for a moment, then spoke again. "Tell me something, Cuddles."

"That is not my name."

"Humor me," said Matthews.

"What must I tell you?"

"Do you ever wonder if there's a God?"

"No, Gar," replied the ship. "Never."

"Or if anything external to the universe you know influences you?"

"I am influenced by cosmic conditions, my internal mechanisms, and human orders."

"And nothing more?"

"No, Gar, nothing more."

"You know the mission I'm on," continued Matthews. "What do you think of it?"

"I do not think of it at all, except as it influences those orders you issue."

"So you have no opinion as to whether Jesus was a man or a god?"

"Yes I do."

"Oh?"

"He was killed. By the definitions in all my dictionaries, that makes him a man."

"And you'd feel the same about anyone who was crucified on any other world—that if they could be killed, then they couldn't be gods?"

"That is correct."

"Interesting," said Matthews.

"Do you disagree, Gar?"

"No," said Matthews. "No, I suppose not." He paused. "It makes you wonder, though."

"Wonder about what?"

"Why we're outnumbered a few billion to one just among my race, and who the hell knows how much more when you toss in the Kauslings and the Shemrees, the Ralti, and all the rest of them."

8

Matthews was met by a huge Shemree as he walked down the ramp from his ship.

"You are Matthews," it said through its translating device. It was not a question.

"Right. And you are–?"

"Follow me," said the Shemree.

"Have you got a name?" asked Matthews as he fell into step behind the alien.

"Yes," was his answer.

He decided there was no use trying to start a conversation, so he simply followed the burly Shemree as it led him through the spaceport, where he saw a few visitors of other races but no Men. Then they were outside, riding a slidewalk to the city center, transferring to another and then a third, and finally stepping off in front of a large building.

There was an inscription above the doorway, but of course Matthews couldn't read it. The doorway itself could accommodate a being twice as high as the Shemree, and he wondered just what kind of aliens came here, There were no windows that he could see, no decorations though the building itself was made of a very rough stone. There were three stairs leading to the doorway, and the instant he entered three more stairs leading back down to ground level.

The artificial lighting had a pinkish glow to it, but try as he might Matthews couldn't spot its source. He found himself in a foyer, the ceiling of which was perhaps two hundred feet high. As he looked around for doors or windows on higher levels he could find none. It was mildly disorienting for a moment, but he was not inexperienced in visiting alien worlds with alien structures and aesthetics, and he waited calmly for his guide to lead him to whoever he was going to interview.

Finally the guide turned to his left, and took him to an airlift – a floorless elevator where they floated gently upward on a cushion of air – and stepped out after a moment. Matthews couldn't begin to guess the floor level or number, but estimated they were about ninety feet above the ground.

They walked down a long, featureless corridor, passed a door at the end of it, turned right, came to another door, and entered. A Shemree, about half the size of the guide, was seated as a desk.

"This is the Matthews," announced the guide.

"Thank you," said the smaller Shemree. "Wait outside for us."

The guide left the office without another word.

"My name is Gar Matthews," said Matthews.

"I know," answered the Shemree. "And I am Bai Hsang Meklo, You may call me Hsang. Won't you sit down?"

Matthews was about to ask where, when a chair suddenly emerged from the floor right next to him.

"Thank you," he said.

The Shemree studied him for a moment. "Forgive me for staring," he said suddenly. "But I've always wondered what you were like."

"Just like any other Man, I should imagine."

"No," said Hsang. "No other Man's work is forbidden to us. Well, *almost* no other Man." He paused. "You do not look dangerous."

"I never raise my hand in anger," said Matthews. Then he smiled. "Just my voice."

"That can usually do more harm," agreed Hsang. "Well, what can I do for you, Gar Matthews?"

"You can answer some questions about an incident that took place in your planet's past," replied Matthews. He frowned. "I don't mean to be rude, but except for your name I have no idea who I'm talking do. May I ask why you have been chosen as my contact here?"

"I am an historian, specializing in the Craimito Era. I have been given to understand that is the historical period that a member of your race will most likely wish to ask about?"

"I assume so."

"You don't know?" asked Hsang, surprised.

"I know what I want to find out," replied Matthews with a smile. "I don't know the name of the era."

"Ah!" said Hsang, and then simply stared at him without saying anything more.

"My understanding," began Matthews, "the reason I'm here, is that you have a major religion that seems to have been created or established, or perhaps codified, when a member of your race was crucified."

"Stop!" said Hsang harshly.

"Yes?" said Matthews curiously.

"If your purpose is an article that attempts to disprove or even belittle our religion, this interview is over."

Matthews shook his head. "That is absolutely not my intention. In fact, I was totally unaware not only of your religion but of your race's existence as recently as three days ago."

Hsang stared at him. "Truly?"

"Truly."

"Then continue."

"Three thousand years ago a man was crucified on Earth, which is the birthplace of *my* race. He was a good and moral man, and he had his followers, but it was that single act of brutality that seemed to give birth to a religion that is based on his teachings and the assumption of his divinity. It is a religion that began as a very small cult, and now numbers perhaps eight or nine billion on Earth and perhaps two hundred colonized worlds."

"Interesting," said Hsang.

"We thought he was unique. Not only that his death precipitated the founding of a religion, but that he was actually crucified. That is an unusual form of execution."

"Ah!" said Hsang with what Matthews interpreted as a smile, and even his translated "Ah!" sounded somehow satisfied. "And you have been to Kaus, have you not?"

Matthews nodded and returned the smile. "Yes. And that led me to here."

"Of course," agreed Hsang. "You know," he added, "I have been waiting for years for *some*one – I didn't know it would be a Man – to come here and ask the very questions you want to know." He paused, looking quite proud of himself. "I *knew* it!"

"So what can you tell me about it?" asked Matthews.

"There was a member of the royalty – we had royalty back then," began Hsang. "His name was Glain Beeyo, and he was cast out into the wilderness by siblings and relatives who resented the fact that he had been given more power than them. So he wandered the land, and wherever he went he made people's lives better, he performed miracles. Not huge, planet-transforming miracles, but the small kinds that affected those whom he befriended. The day came when he had so many followers that they stormed the residences of the royalty, killed most of them, and exiled the rest, and begged him to become the Emperor."

"Let me guess," said Matthews. "He refused the honor."

"He refused it," confirmed Hsang. "He also refused to kill the surviving royalty, and that was his only mistake, for they gathered in their exile, put together an armed force, returned to their former homes – you would call them palaces – and jailed and eventually crucified him." He paused. "They had far more efficient means of execution, but none as long and painful, and they had been carrying their hatred of him for a long time." Another pause. "It wasn't too long before the people overthrew and killed what was left of the royalty, and began teaching what he had taught them all across the world. I don't think it was a religion, as such, for a century or more, but eventually it became one, Beeyo was worshipped, his teachings were codified as if he were the spokesperson for God or perhaps was God himself. And as we developed space flight and began reaching other worlds, we spread Beeyo's teachings, first to the two other inhabited planets in what you know as the Beta Piscium system, and then on to other systems."

"Including Kaus?" asked Matthews.

"Kaus was a failure," answered Hsang. "And I suspect you know why."

Matthews smiled. "They had their own religion, based on the teachings of a crucified martyr."

"Precisely. They actually killed some of our religious teachers for the crime of blaspheming." Hsang paused. "Of course, we killed even more of them. We were better armed, and we were protecting ourselves. But eventually we realized that continual contact with them would simply result in more violence, which is against Beeyo's teachings, so we left."

"I can sympathize with your position," said Matthews wryly. "We've killed more than our share of people in Christ's name."

"Now let me ask you," said Hsang. "What is the purpose of your research, the hoped-for result?"

"I won't know until I'm finished," admitted Matthews. "A month ago not a single member of my race knew that any other race's major religion came about through similar, if not identical circumstances, to Christianity. We felt – hell, ninety-nine percent of us still feel – that our religion is unique."

"What purpose will be served by proving that it is *not* unique?" asked Hsang.

Matthews grimaced. "It's kind of difficult to explain."

"Please try," said Hsang. "I find this fascinating."

"I'm not sure I've really thought it through," replied Matthews. "I have always been an atheist. I think religion creates an artificial authority to get people to behave in reasonable, moral ways – though I'll admit that Christianity isn't the only religion among my people, and some of our religions are as brutal and barbaric as you'll find anywhere in the galaxy. But Christianity has, over the millennia, become the major religion of my race."

"A religion in which you do not believe."

"That's right."

"Then I do not understand."

"I believe in its precepts," continued Matthews. "Most of them, anyway. In a perfect world I'd probably believe in all of them."

"I still do not understand," said the Shemree.

"I believe in the precepts, not the authority."

"Not God and not this Jesus," said Hsang.

"Right. It seems like a fluke that crucifying a decent man should have created a religion that has grown to what it has become today." He paused. "But if I can show that a *lot* of religions on a number of worlds have also come about because on each of them a moral member of the native race was crucified or the equivalent, that opens things up to a lot of serious speculation."

"That God has chosen a disciple on each world," said Hsang promptly.

"Or that if and when these very decent notions occur to a member of a relatively unsophisticated race, a race that has not yet achieved the level of sophistication or civilization that it is destined to achieve, the most common response to such notions at that stage of a society's development is crucifixion." He paused. "That would tend to take religion out of the equation."

Hsang stared at him for a long moment. "I think you are due to be disappointed," he said.

"Oh?" replied Matthews. "About what?"

Hsang shrugged. "If I am right, you will know, and if I am wrong, it is not worth mention. May I ask where your next port of call will be?"

"A world named Greenbriar."

"Ah!" said Hsang. "Wiskinti VII."

"Yes, that's correct." Matthews paused. "Knowing about these other systems and their religions doesn't seem to have had any effect on yours."

"One believes or one doesn't," answered Hsang. "I will have a history of our religion transmitted to your ship."

"I don't know if it can translate it into Terran."

Hsang indicated his translating device that rested on his left shoulder. "I am speaking Terran. The history will arrive in Terran."

"I thank you."

Hsang stared at him for a long minute. "Tell me that a year from now."

9

"Sure as hell doesn't look green from here," commented Matthews as he stared at the viewscreen.

"You're looking at the nightside of the planet," replied the ship.

"So what's it like? Do I need any special equipment?"

"You might want an additional outer garment. The mean temperature where I'm preparing to land is 7.2 degrees Celsius, or 45 degrees Fahrenheit, or—"

"Enough!" muttered Matthews. "I got the picture. What about the rest of the stuff?"

"Gravity, 1.03 Standard, atmosphere 97% Standard. The three percent difference is entirely composed of inert elements."

"Good," said Matthews. "I guess they only crucify holy men on oxygen planets."

"Not so," said the ship. "I have already found seven chlorine worlds and two methane worlds where—"

"Yeah, I know. It was just a thing to say." A pause. "So did we have an embassy here?"

"Yes, Gar."

"Okay, they can show me around and set up a meeting."

"No, Gar."

Matthews frowned. "What are you talking about?"

"Evidently some of your columns have so offended the Ambassador that he has ordered his staff not to help you in any way."

"Are you sure?"

"They just told me so seventeen minutes ago."

"Screw 'em," said Matthews. "Find me a guide who speaks Terran."

"Checking…no member of the Ralti speaks Terran."

"How the hell does the embassy speak to them?"

"Through translating mechanisms."

"Shit!"

"I have portable translating mechanisms, Gar."

"What good is that if they're not programmed for Ralti?" demanded Matthews.

"Checking," said the ship. "Their mechanisms have five languages in common with ours. You won't be conversing in Ralti or Terran, but each will translate the language you use into the user's native language."

"Cuddles, I take back all the nasty things I was thinking about you."

"Thank you," said the ship. "And my name is not Cuddles."

"Neither is mine, but I'd never tell a beautiful woman not to call me that."

The ship restrained itself from pointing out that Matthews was not a beautiful woman.

"Well?" demanded Matthews after a moment. "What's taking so long?"

"I will not land for twenty-six minutes, Gar. You know that."

"Yeah, but you always tell me where we're landing and who I'm meeting."

"I do not know."

"Why the hell not?" said Matthews. "Just tell 'em I want to talk with a priest, or maybe a religious historian. You know the routine."

"I have said that," replied the ship. "It took an extra ten minutes to get permission to land."

"What are you talking about?"

"This is not like the last two worlds, Gar," said the ship. "The religion you seek to learn about has been outlawed here, and the practitioners are all in hiding."

"They're legally criminals?"

"Yes."

"And the religion doesn't require wild orgies or the equivalent of human sacrifice?"

"Not as far as I can tell."

"Let me take a guess," said Matthews. "It's less than two centuries old."

"I've no idea. No one will discuss it with me, except to say that it is illegal. They were very reluctant to let me land until I convinced them that you were not a practitioner."

"How did you pull that off?"

"I showed them some of your more controversial columns."

Matthews looked dubious. "How does a ship know which are my most controversial columns?"

"I selected the ones that provoked the most lawsuits and death threats."

"Thanks a heap, Brutus."

"My name is not Brutus."

Matthews walked over to his cot and slid a trunk out from beneath it. He opened it, rummaged clumsily through it, and pulled out a fur-lined jacket.

"Tell me that the Ralti aren't covered with fur," he said.

"They are not," replied the ship.

"Okay, I'm set, then." He returned to his chair.

"Message coming in," announced the ship.

"Put it on audio."

"There's no sense doing that," replied the ship. "It's not in Terran."

"Fine. Tell me what it said when they're done babbling."

A moment later the transmission ended.

"Well?" said Matthews.

"I am landing at the spaceport in the city of Quentrelk."

"Wherever and whatever *that* is."

"Quentrelk has a population of just under two million, and is the capital of the city-state of Quentresakot."

"Okay, we're landing in an unpronounceable location in an unpronounceable city-state. What else?"

"You will be met by an official of the government."

"Has he got a name?" asked Matthews.

"Almost certainly," responded the ship. "But they did not divulge it to me."

"Okay, I'll find out when I get there."

"One more thing."

"Oh?"

"They suggest that you bring along a hand weapon if you possess one."

Matthews looked his surprise. "A hand weapon?"

"That is my translation. The translating mechanism actually called it a sidearm."

"Are they at war?" asked Matthews.

"Not a formal war, no," replied the ship.

"Okay, it's an informal war. With who?"

"With the very people you are here to learn about."

10

Matthews emerged from the ship, and immediately noticed the chill in the air. And the chill wasn't only from the seven degrees Celsius. There were a plethora of armed, uniformed beings forming a brief line from the ship to the Customs building.

Even though he'd known, in a general way, what the Ralti looked like, the actually sight of them still surprised Matthews. The trunks of their bodies – one couldn't call them torsos – extended some two to two and one-half meters from side to side, and another meter from top to bottom. Their heads, which seemed as close to canine as human, sat atop long, thin necks, and could swivel about 120 degrees in either direction. They had six short stubby legs, and four somewhat longer, more flexible arms.

They looked, thought Matthews, as if a very bad cartoonist had tried to create a being that was not quite funny, a bit short of horrifying, and totally incapable of existing – yet there they were, lining his path.

Since they were clearly a police or military force, he felt an urge to salute, but any sudden move could be misinterpreted, especially if they hadn't seen many Men before, so he simply walked down the line and entered the Customs building.

There was only a single operative booth, and there were three beings, all of races he did not recognize, ahead of him, but within ten minutes he had had the ID chip that was embedded in his neck scanned and okayed, answered a few general questions, and then passed through.

Just as he was wondering where to go or what to do next, he was approaching by a Raltor who was wearing what passed for civilian clothes, which was to say, no discernable weapons.

"Gar Matthews?" came the translated voice.

"Yes," said Matthews. "And your name is?"

The Raltor made a face and pointed to Matthews' translating mechanism.

"Sorry," said Matthews after activating it. "Are you my guide?"

"I am your..." The translating mechanism clearly couldn't translate the next word. "I am your everything," said the Raltor, trying again.

"Have you a name?"

"Of course I do," was the reply. "I am Tench Brikali."

"I am pleased to meet you," said Matthews. He considered extending his hand, saw too many of Tench Brikali's hands confronting him, and decided against it. "You know why I am here?"

"To learn why we make war against the despised Vordi."

"Vordi?" repeated Matthews, frowning.

"Vordi," confirmed Tench Brikali. "Those who gnaw at the very foundations of our civilization."

"Yes, that is why I am here."

"Have you this same problem on your world?"

Say yes and he'll spend the rest of your time on the planet picking your *mind,* thought Matthews. *Say no and he'll assume you're a liar, because no one comes this far to learn about a local war in a minor system.*

"It is possible," said Matthews at last. "From what I have learned there are some similarities. That is why I need to learn more."

"I shall do my best," replied Tench Brikali.

Good. You bought it.

"Have you some place where we can go?"

"Certainly," replied the Raltor. "You cannot teleport, can you?"

"No."

"That will not be a problem. Almost no races other than my own can." He paused in thought for a moment. "I think first I will take you to the museum."

"That sounds interesting," commented Matthews. "Lead the way. I will follow you."

"We will not walk there. It is too far."

Tench Brikali led Matthews out the exit to what looked like a flat sled on a dozen small wheels.

"Step aboard."

Matthews climbed onto the sled. "Is there anything to hold onto?"

The Raltor looked puzzled. "Why?"

"If it should make a sharp turn or come to a sudden stop, I might fall off," replied Matthews. "I do not have as many legs as you do."

"I see," said Tench Brikali. "I will instruct the machine to take that into account."

The machine thinks? Or is he just saying he'll drive carefully.

"Thank you."

Matthews tried to ignore the cold wind as the sled rolled along the street, past row upon row of buildings that were shaped like anything *but* buildings. Some had no discernable entrances, others had dozens of doors of varying shapes and sizes, some were windowless, some were made entirely of glass or some other transparent material. Streets curved back upon themselves, or widened by adding numerous extra lanes and then dead-ended half a block later. Ralti pedestrians popped into and out of existence as they teleported to and from the street. As used as Matthews was to alien cities, this one seemed more alien than most.

Finally, after about five minutes – it was easier to judge the time spent than the distance covered – the sled slowed, and soon reached a stop in front of a long low building. Matthews stared at it and concluded that it must be a building for midgets, that the ceiling couldn't be much more than four feet above the ground.

"We have arrived," announced Tench Brikali, stepping down onto what passed for the pavement.

Matthews followed suit, and the Raltor led him to the front door, which was wide enough to accommodate the locals but seemed to leave them no head room. The door seemed to vanish as they approached it, and the Raltor and Matthews stepped onto a platform that lowered them a dozen feet below ground level. They stepped off it into a huge, artificially-lighted area that extended for hundreds of feet in each direction, even under the street, and the ceiling was now some twenty feet above them.

"Impressive," remarked Matthews.

"This way," said Tench Brikali, heading off to his right.

They passed a dozen stuffed and mounted animals that bore no resemblance to any animal Matthews had ever seen, and a number of machines and inventions that, whether primitive or sophisticated in design, were all unknown to him.

Suddenly they came to a separate room where only the display cases were lit, and the rest was totally dark.

"Come," said Tench Brikali, leading Matthews into the room.

And then they came to it: a life-sized representation of a Raltor, bleeding from dozens of wounds, nailed to the same strangely-shaped structure that Matthews had seen in miniature on Beta Piscium II.

"That's *him*?" he asked.

"Yes," answered Tench Brikali.

"What was his name?"

"Zababa Zenoital."

"There's a little plaque behind his head what some writing on it," continued Matthews.

"Yes."

"What does it say?"

"They are just initials in a dead language," replied Tench Brikali.

"How long ago was he crucified?"

"My translating mechanism has some difficulty with that word."

"How long ago was he killed?"

"173 years."

"That's not that long."

"In another 173 years he will be totally forgotten."

I wouldn't bet on it, thought Matthews. Aloud he said: "What exactly were his crimes?"

"Blasphemy. Insurrection. Treason," answered the Raltor.

"That's quite a catalog."

"And a true one. Thanks to him, we are plagued with the despised Vordi."

"Tell me about it, and him."

"Not here," replied Tench Brikali. "I find it oppressive to be in his presence, or even that of a facsimile."

"Anywhere you want."

"There is a restaurant on the premises, but I think you would draw too much attention. We will go to my dwelling."

"Sounds good to me."

They retraced their steps, and were soon riding the sled through the cold air to what seemed to be the outskirts of the city. Finally it stopped, they stepped off it, and the Raltor led Matthews to a small building that was every bit as odd as the others they had passed. This one seemed shaped like a tire or an inner tube, and except for a single door was every bit as airtight, with not a single window in the entire structure.

"Is this all yours?" asked Matthews, who felt it could easily hold thirty of more Ralti without feeling cramped.

"No," answered Tench Brikali. "There are four others. But they will not bother us."

He led Matthews down a broad, illuminated corridor that followed the contour of the tire, and in about ten yards came to some furniture that was clearly created to accommodate the Ralti.

"Collapse," said Tench Brikali.

Matthews assumed that was as close as the translating mechanism could come to "Sit", and he sat down on the edge of an uneven bench. The Raltor sat – *sprawled* was more the word – on another well-worn piece of furniture.

"And now we shall talk about Zababa Zenoital and the despised Vordi."

"Yes, please," replied Matthews.

"We were a peaceful, contented society before he came along," began Tench Brikali. "Not everyone fared as well, but no one went hungry. We had rulers, and warriors, and merchants, and farmers, and laborers, like every society. We were not perfect yet, but we were nearing perfection, and many of our people felt we could achieve it within their lifetimes." He paused, and his expression hardened. "And then *he* came along."

The Raltor seemed to be waiting for a response for Matthews, so he said, "You mean Zababa Zenoital?"

"The demon," confirmed Tench Brikali. "He challenged everything: the laws, the wars, the right of the rulers to rule. We had experienced such radicals before, but they had never claimed to speak in the name of the deity."

"And he did?"

"He did that, and worse."

"For example?" asked Matthews.

"He healed the sick."

"Why would you want to kill someone like that, whatever he believed?"

"Because he would perform his miracles only upon those who pledged to disobey the law and instead follow his precepts."

"Did he actually perform miracles, or did he simply possess an advanced knowledge of medicine that had not yet been discovered by other healers in your society?"

"His followers swore to his miracles," answered Tench Brikali. "They were lying, of course."

"Of course," said Matthews. "So they all died, all the ones who supposedly underwent miracle cures?"

"They are all dead," said the Raltor noncommittally.

Of course they're all dead – now, thought Matthews. Aloud he said: "Now, who are these Vordi you've mentioned?"

"His followers. Originally there were merely a few, but as he traveled the land, preaching his vitriol, the Vordi's numbers increased. Finally, when he refused to alter his positions despite our peaceful overtures, the government had no choice but to eliminate him."

"So they crucified him."

"That word again," said the Raltor, staring at his translating mechanism.

"They nailed his limbs to a structure, as we saw in the museum."

"Yes."

"But that didn't end the problem," noted Matthews.

"No, it did not. The Despised Vordi multiply like—" The translating mechanism couldn't give him a Terran equivalent of the next word, though Matthews suspected it was "flies."

"And you are at war with them?"

"It is a most unusual war," answered Tench Brikali.

"In what way?" asked Matthews.

"They do not fight."

"Then it is not a war."

"It *is*!" insisted the Raltor.

"Explain, please," said Matthews.

"They do not fight, that is true," came the reply. "But they do not *obey*! Ever! And they recruit, and recruit, and recruit! No matter how many we kill, more show up to take their place." Tench Brikali paused a moment to control his emotions. "You would think it is not a war when your enemy does not meet you in battle. But when they convince farmers not to grow crops so that the established order will have little to eat, when they will not obey any order that contradicts the teachings of Zababa Zenoital in any way, when they risk their own lives to hide criminals who have broken our laws…well, you can see for yourself. We are living in an armed, militarized state, all thanks to that wretched creature whose likeness you saw in the museum – he who spoke of love and peace, and caused nothing but hate and war!"

"So how do you punish someone who can teleport away?" asked Matthews.

"We can only teleport when we concentrate."

"And?" asked Matthews, feeling there had to be a second half of the statement.

"And we cannot concentrate when we are in discomfort or pain. So we shoot or otherwise cripple the Vordi when we find them, and then attach them to the structure, where they are in such pain that they remain where they are until they expire."

"I have just a few more questions," said Matthews. "How large is your planetary population?"

"Six hundred million."

"And how many Vordi are there?"

"Perhaps four million. Possibly less."

Even if you're not lying downward, you've gone from a handful to four million. I don't think even Christianity spread that fast.

"A last question," said Matthews. "Have the Vordis codified their beliefs, perhaps in a book that they pass from one to another?"

Tench Brikali looked surprised. "There are rumors of such a book," he answered. "But I have never seen it, nor do I know any Ralti who has." Suddenly he stopped and stared at Matthews. "So has your world experienced our particular situation?"

"Parts of it."

"Your presence here means that you solved it," continued the Raltor. "I find it encouraging that you killed all of your Vordi. It means that we can do the same."

"I've learned just about everything I can learn from Greenbriar," said Matthews, getting to his feet. "I hate to further impose upon you, but could you take me back to my ship?"

"It is no imposition at all," replied Tench Brikali. "You have no idea how greatly you have encouraged me…*us*."

Matthews was on his ship twenty minutes later, preparing to take off. He pulled the museum up on his viewscreen and stared at it as the ship began moving.

Too bad I don't believe in messiahs, he thought, remembering the creature on its equivalent of a cross, *because otherwise you'd damn well qualify as one in the making.*

II

"Well," remarked Matthews, looking at the planetary readout on the screen, "I figure we can skip this one."

"Why?" asked the ship. "According to my records, it fulfills all your criteria: it is populated, the population is sentient, a very special member of the society was singled out for punishment and not one but two viable religions have evolved, both tracing their roots back to him."

"Makes no difference," replied Matthews. "Head to the next one on the list."

"But this world—"

"Forget it," said Matthews. "It's a methane world."

"Surely you are not suggesting that sentient life cannot evolve and thrive on a methane world."

"Of course I'm not suggesting that. Happy now?"

"I have no emotions," said the ship. "But I do have curiosity."

"I would never have guessed."

"And I do not have sarcasm."

"Too bad," said Matthews. "It's just what you need for conversing with an uppity ship."

"I am yours to command," said the ship. "I am compelled by my programming to go where you tell me to go, and perform those duties you assign me. But I truly wish to know why we are turning away from Tchandral XII."

"Okay," said Matthews. "What kind of beings live on methane worlds?"

"It depends on the world."

"On Tchandral XII?"

"Crystalline bipeds," said the ship.

"Well, there you have it," said Matthews.

"There I have *what?*"

"What happens when you nail a crystalline biped to a cross?"

"He suffers, I would assume."

Matthews shook his head. "Guess again."

"I don't know what you are driving at," complained the ship.

"He *shatters!*" snapped Matthews. "He doesn't maintain his structural integrity long enough to utter a single sentence. No one who shows up ten seconds later will be able to relate how he suffered, or to repeat any last words he had to offer."

"Ah!" said the ship. "I see."

"So let's head off to the next one on the list. This would have been a total waste of time, and while you'll still be functioning at peak efficiency in two or three centuries, there's an expiration date on human bodies."

"Yes, Gar."

"So where are we going now?"

"Bendoti III."

"Just tell me it's not an ice world," said Matthews. "I hate snow and ice. Hell, Greenbriar was cold enough."

"It is not an ice world, Gar."

"Is that the truth, or did you say it because I told you to?"

"Both," answered the ship.

"Good," said Matthews. "At least I won't be cold."

"No, Gar," said the ship. "You won't be cold."

※

Matthews trudged through the swamp, laser pistol in hand, prepared to shoot anything with teeth and more than two legs that approached to within fifty feet. He was drenched, not from the swamp water, which was only eighteen inches deep where he was, but from the sweat that had been caused by the almost unbearable heat and humidity.

Finally he came to the spot he'd pinpointed from the ship, a peninsula that offered almost no shade. A few hundred yards away he could see a small city, and again cursed the fact that the ship weighed too much to have landed there, that it would have sunk right into the soft ground had it not landed on a rocky outcropping two miles behind him.

A few members of the local race were approaching him, and he decided it was time to holster his weapon before they concluded that he meant them any harm.

As they came closer he could see that the bipedal beings were wearing several layers of clothing, more than he would have thought necessary.

They offered him a friendly greeting. His translating mechanism took a few moments to analyze and program their language, but soon he was able to speak with them. They seemed amazed that an extra-planetary being had come to visit them again.

"Again?" asked Matthews.

Oh, yes, they responded. They had been visited before, three separate times, in the past. They were gracious hosts, they opened their doors (not that they had any) and their hearts to their visitors, and indeed had hoped to be gifted with the secret of interstellar travel so that they could join the thriving galactic community.

And then *he* had shown up.

Who were they referring to, Matthews wanted to know.

It was of no import, they replied. He has been dead for a long time.

Matthews tried again to get them to talk about what he assumed was their Messiah figure, but they were much more interested in learning about his race and the likelihood of more visits from other galactics.

Finally he mentioned that the reason he was so interested in the zealot who had died was that he thought one of his followers had found his way to Matthews' world.

Impossible, said the beings of Bendoti III. We do not have space travel.

He claimed that this was where he came from, insisted Matthews, and indeed he looked like a member of your race.

What was his name, they asked. What did he call our world?

Matthews tiptoed around the questions, claiming that it had all been lost in translation. The only thing he was sure of was the being's beliefs. Could they tell him something of their enemy's beliefs and let him see if they compared.

And finally they did so.

The story was about what Matthews had expected, since it was pretty much the same story he'd encountered on the last three worlds he'd been to: The non-military defiance, the lectures, the parables, the growth of the being's followers, his crucifixion, and the establishment of a religion, or at least a set of principles, stemming from a belief in what he stood for, or perhaps what he was.

And did this compare with the being Matthews had encountered, they wanted to know.

No, said Matthews, he had been mistaken.

His hosts breathed a collective sigh of relief. It was bad enough on *this* world, trying to maintain the established order in the face of his growing number of followers. They didn't want to be responsible for it spreading to any other world.

He reassured them that this was not the case, allowed them to escort him to a shaded area when they offered his some bitter but welcome liquids to drink, and as night fell and he had regained some of his strength two of them walked him back to his ship.

They pledged eternal friendship to each other, and then he was back inside the vessel and wondering why he had ever objected to ice worlds.

⁂

"Next on the list is Troonskor XVI," announced the ship.

"Throw it up on the screen and let me see what it's like. Not just the visual, but a readout of all the vital signs."

"A patient has vital signs, Gar," the ship corrected him. "A planet does not have any."

"Fine," said Matthews. "Show me it's gravity, surface, atmosphere, and temperature for starters. Then I'll tell you what else I need."

"Working...done."

Matthews surveyed the screen and frowned. "Ugly, rocky place."

"Well, it *is* six hundred million miles from its sun," said the ship.

"Chlorine atmosphere?"

"Correct."

"So how the hell do we know if they've gone around crucifying anyone?" persisted Matthews. "We've only got six or seven populated chlorine worlds in the whole damned galaxy."

"This is what I found, Gar."

"Gravity three times normal?"

"Three point one six," answered the ship.

"And their noon is about as bright as the last couple of minutes of our twilight."

"That is basically correct," agreed the ship.

"Who the hell would want to live here?"

"Those who were born here."

"It's about as uninviting a populated world as I've seen," said Matthews. He frowned. "You're sure they fit my specifications?"

"Yes, Gar, they seem to."

"Did you speak directly to anyone on the planet, or did you read it in some report?"

"It was mentioned by the Benvenuti Expedition of 3392 A.D., Gar."

"So you don't even know what language the locals use?"

"According to the expedition, they use eleven, depending of their location."

"Wonderful," muttered Matthews. "So I can't get out of my spacesuit, I can't speak to the locals without a translating device (and you know how badly they work with chlorine breathers), and I'm going to feel like I'm walking around with a lead trunk on each foot and a half-ton boulder on my back." He grimaced. "But except for all that I'll be just fine."

"That is correct, Gar."

"Bendoti III didn't have a spaceport. Does this world?"

"Yes, Gar. Just one."

"Good. So they have to make contact with incoming ships."

"Yes."

"So we should be able to communicate with them."

"Yes, Gar. It will be much easier through my control panel than for you once you are on the planet."

"Okay," said Matthews, leaning back on his chair. "Contact them, tell them we'd like landing coordinates, and when they ask what our purpose for visiting them is – and they *always* ask – turn the communications over to me."

"Yes, Gar." A moment later the ship said: "They wish to speak to you, Gar."

"Fine. I hate earphones. Put it on audio."

"Done."

"Hello?" said Matthews.

"Please state your name, your ship's identification code, and your purpose for visiting Unchlator."

"Unchlator?"

"That is the name of this planet."

"Oh," said Matthews. "Okay, my name is Gar Matthews. My ship will transmit its ID to you" – he waited for a few seconds – "and my purpose for visiting is that I am a writer, and I would like to use your world in a book I am writing."

"Can you assure us that our world will be viewed in a favorable way by readers?" said the emotionless translated voice.

"Yes, I certainly hope so. I have come because the last world I visited had problems that, if honestly presented, would cause my readers to view the government with some hostility."

"Oh?"

"Yes," said Matthews. "But I am sure Unchlator has no problem with religious unrest or public disobedience."

There was a fifteen-second pause. "Religious unrest?"

Matthews allowed himself the luxury of a smile.

"Yes. They killed a religious leader some time back, and have been living with the unpleasant consequences ever since. That is why I have come to your world. I don't fictionalize my backgrounds, so that world is clearly unsuitable for my purposes."

"Please hold your position," said the voice. "I will get back to you shortly."

Matthews gave the ship a thumbs-up sign, then realized that it would have no idea what the sign meant, and just waited patiently. And waited.

And waited.

After fifteen minutes the voice spoke again.

"I am sorry, Gar Matthews, but permission to land is denied "

"If it is a technical problem, I can wait," said Matthews.

"It would be better if you did not."

"All right," replied Matthews. "Perhaps some time in the future."

"Perhaps," said the voice, cutting off communication.

Matthews uttered a triumphant war-whoop. "No space suit, no crushing gravity, no landing at all! You're working with a genius, Cuddles!"

"My name is not Cuddles," replied the ship.

"But you *are* working with a genius," persisted Matthew with a triumphant grin.

The ship made no answer.

Whatever its answer might have been, it was a working relationship that would soon be terminated.

Permanently.

12

Matthews was hurled off his bed into the wall on the other side of the ship. It took him a moment to clear his head and wipe the blood from his face.

"What the hell happened?" he mumbled, spitting out a tooth.

"I was just emerging from the Nesteranko Wormhole and ran into a meteor swarm," replied the ship. "There was no way to see or sense them from within the wormhole."

"How's your structural integrity?" asked Matthews.

"I'm not losing air," said the ship. "But I have sustained serious damage."

"*How* serious?"

"I have lost all motive power, and all ability to make course changes or corrections."

"You mean we're just floating in space and you can't do anything about it?"

"In essence."

"Well, we'll send out an S.O.S. and wait for someone to come along and tug us to a friendly port."

"That will not be possible, Gar," said the ship.

"Why not?"

"My ability to communicate with anything external to myself has been compromised." The ship paused. "And there is another, more immediate problem."

"Oh?" said Matthews.

"Can you see that planet on the screen?"

"No," replied Matthews. "The screen's blank."

"Another ability compromised," said the ship.

"What about the planet?"

"I am headed toward it," answered the ship, "and I no longer have the ability to make course corrections. I will shortly be captured by its gravitational field."

"And there's no way to break free?" asked Matthews, frowning.

"Not under the current circumstance, Gar."

"Are there any large bodies of water on the planet?"

"The planet is Bastion IV," said the ship. "I cannot access my records, but I knew that we would be near the Bastion system when we emerged, so I filed the information away. You will be able to breathe the air and tolerate the gravity."

"Well, let's hope one of the spaceports gets curious when you don't respond to their signals."

"Gar, they don't have a spaceport."

"Not even one?" asked Matthews, frowning again.

"Not even one. They are a sentient race, but they have not yet mastered space travel."

"Shit! Can you maneuver enough to land in an ocean?"

"No, Gar, I cannot."

"How long have we got before you touch down?" asked Matthews.

"Before I crash," the ship corrected him.

"How long?"

"Perhaps twelve minutes."

"That's all?" said Matthews, surprised.

"That is all."

"What can we do to break your fall, to land with less force?"

"Nothing," answered the ship. "You will have to take the lifeboat. I have activated some of its systems. The rest have been inoperative since the collision."

"All right," said Matthews, walking to the unit where the lifeboat was stores. "Open the hatch once we hit the atmosphere. I've got to be able to get out before you crash."

"Yes, Gar."

Matthews walked around the now-misshapen ship, picking up a laser pistol here, a pocket computer there, a backpack that he filled with food from the galley.

"Okay, I'm ready," he said after another minute had passed. "Once I'm on the ground I'll get together with the locals and see what kind of radio I can rig that'll reach some other world, someplace that can send whatever it takes to put you together again."

"I will be damaged beyond repair," replied the ship.

"Maybe not," said Matthews. "I've seen them save disabled ships before."

"Not ships that plunged full force into the ground, Gar."

Matthews was silent for another minute, then looked out the hatch at the planet.

"How much longer?" he asked.

"Less than five minutes," said the ship.

There was another silence, briefer this time.

"Gar?" said the ship.

"Yeah?"

"I'm afraid."

"*Machines* don't have any emotions," said Matthews.

"I don't know what else to call it."

"There's no need to be scared. You can't feel pain."

"I am not afraid of pain," said the ship. "I am afraid of dying."

"You power down between voyages," said Matthews. "That's pretty much the same thing, isn't it?"

"Yes," replied the ship. "But when I power down, I know I'll wake up again, that my memories will be intact, what makes me *me* will not vanish forever."

"I'm sure we'll be able to salvage bits and pieces."

"I am not bits and pieces," said the ship. "I am me, and even as we speak more and more of my functions have vanished forever."

Matthews had no idea how to comfort a frightened ship, so he simply stood near the hatch and remained quiet.

"Four minutes," announced the ship. "Prepare to leave."

Matthews climbed into the lifeboat.

"Three minutes. We are approaching a large forest. Your breaking mechanism is inoperative. It is possible that the branches may slow your descent or break your fall."

"Or my neck, or my back," said Matthews grimly.

"Two minutes and forty seconds...Good-bye, Gar."

"I'll miss you, ship," said Matthews.

"My name is Cuddles," replied the ship.

Matthews took off and immediately plunged down toward a forest of tall blue-tinted trees as the ship crashed noisily to the ground, a molten misshapen mess.

13

He awoke to a strange taste in his mouth, followed by even stranger movement. He was laying on his back, and turned slowly and very painfully onto his left side, opened his mouth and half-blew, half-spit out an ugly ten-legged insect.

He lay still for a few minutes, taking stock of all his body parts. The arms were sore as hell, but they worked. So, finally, did the fingers. He was pretty sure one of his legs was in a bad way, but he couldn't tell which one yet.

He looked around for the ship, but couldn't spot it. Another insect began crawling across his cheek toward his eye. He tried to brush it off with a hand, grunted in pain when he attempted to reach the insect, and settled for closing his eye. Finally his hand responded to his will, and he flicked the insect onto the ground.

After an indeterminate length of time, which he guessed could have been anywhere from ten minutes to an hour, he managed to get to a kneeling position. He crawled painfully to a small tree some twelve feet away, grabbed the narrow trunk, and slowly, laboriously pulled himself up to a standing position.

He looked around for the ship, though he didn't expect it to be anywhere near him, and indeed it wasn't. He took a tentative step, grunted in pain, and fell heavily to the ground.

He waited until his head cleared, then pulled himself to his feet again. The mere fact that he could put weight on both feet led him to conclude that neither leg was broken.

"Well, I can't just stand here forever," he muttered, and took a very tentative, very painful step, then another and another. Within an hour he had progressed almost fifty yards, and emerged into a small clearing. Fifty yards an hour wasn't much, and there was nothing in the clearing but golden ground cover and a few innocuous-looking lizards, but he nonetheless felt an enormous sense of accomplishment.

One of the trees had some orange-tinted fruit on a low-hanging branch. He wasn't hungry, but he didn't know when he'd see anything else that looked remotely edible, so he hobbled over to the branch and pulled off a trio of the fruits, stuffing two in his pockets.

"Might as well find out now," he half-whispered, and took a bite of the third. "Tastes okay," he muttered. "Now let's see if it kills me."

He waited for the fruit to have a deleterious effect, but he was already in so much pain that he couldn't tell if he was suddenly suffering from even more. He took two more bites, tossed what was left to a purple lizard that had been eyeing it since he picked it off the branch, and began making his way painfully across the clearing.

He had no idea where he was going, just that he felt he had to keep moving, that rest and sleep seemed so attractive that he was sure if he lay down there was a fair chance he'd never get up again. So he walked, agonizing step by agonizing step. Night fell, but the world's three moons illuminated the trees enough for him to continue making his way through them, and by morning he'd made it totally out of the forest and onto a broad golden plain.

He decided to stop and take a quick inventory of his wounds. He knew he had a deep gash on his forehead, because it had kept bleeding into his eye until half an hour ago. Both his knees and one of his ankles were swollen and incredibly painful whether he was moving or not. He was pretty sure he'd broken his right wrist, plus a couple of fingers on his right hand. His left shoulder seemed all right as long as he didn't use it, but lifting his left arm caused it so much agony that he tried only once and not again. He knew he'd lost a few teeth – some when he landed, and another when he bit into the fruit – but the rest seemed intact. His eyes were functioning, and he didn't have any trouble breathing, which implied that his ribs were intact.

On any civilized world I'd spend the next month in a hospital, he thought wryly. *I wonder how many miles I can go before I collapse – and once I do, if I'll ever get up again?*

He began walking again, until the pain overwhelmed him. He had meant only to sit down and rest for a while, but he had obviously fallen asleep, because when he opened his eyes he found himself confronting four humanoid figures, each of them pointing a spear at him.

14

The figure that was closest to him said something, but of course Matthews had no idea what it was, so he shrugged, trying to ignore the pain that caused, and held his hands out, palms up. The Bastion native said something else, ending on an upnote, which Matthews assumed was indicative of a question.

"Gar," he said. "Gar Matthews."

"Gargar," repeated the being.

Matthews forced a smile to his cracked lips. "Gar Matthews," he said.

"Garmat," said the being.

What the hell, thought Matthews, *It's close enough.*

"Garmat," he agreed.

The being tapped himself on the chest. "Bligori."

Matthews pointed very slowly at him. "Bligori?"

Bligori responded with what Matthews assumed was a smile, and uttered a full sentence, ending in another upnote.

"I wish I could understand you," said Matthews. "But I don't. Here, let me get up."

He tried to rise. When he started to fall over to his left, two of the Bastion beings caught him and righted him.

"Thank you," he said, forcing himself to smile again.

Bligori said something else, turned, and began walking slowly away. Matthew started to follow him, sure he would collapse in the first few strides, but his two supporters held him upright, seemed to determine how fast he could walk without groaning in pain, and called ahead to Bligori, who slowed his pace to accommodate the human.

It was the most difficult hour of Matthews' life, but at last they came to a village of perhaps three dozen reed dwellings, each a perfect rectangle. There was a thorn fence around the village, which was also rectangular. Bligori led Matthews and his living crutches to a nearby dwelling and indicated that he should enter it.

Matthews did so, found a very soft sleeping mat laid out against a side wall, took a tentative step toward it, and when no one stopped him he went over and very gently lowered himself onto it.

"Thank you for your hospitality, Bligori," he said.

Bligori answered in gentle tones, called him Garmat again, and left the hut. A moment later two smaller members of Bligori's race entered. They possessed developed breasts, which implied that the species was mammalian in nature. They approached him, studying him carefully.

"If I'm in your house, I can always move," said Matthews.

They smiled at him, conferred in very low tones with each other, and then produced some treated cloths and began very gently cleaning his wounds. Every time he groaned or winced they stopped and stared at him as if he was some delicate piece of crystal that might shatter any moment.

"I must be more banged up than I thought," he grated. "You two don't look like you expect me to last out the morning – or whatever the hell time of day it is." They continued working on him, and while he wasn't feeling any better when they finished an hour later, he had to admit that he was considerably cleaner.

He exchanged names with them, and with anyone else who entered the structure. As long as he was stuck here, probably for years, quite possibly for the rest of his life, he might as well start learning not only names but how to speak with them.

15

And so he learned the language, and some of the customs, and the landscape, and he did it faster than he ever thought he could – but, as he kept pointing out to himself, when you have no alternative, you learn in a hurry.

The first thing he learned was that the inhabitants of Bastion IV called their world Goldenblue – which made sense, since the predominant colors were the gold of the vegetation and the blue of the multitude of oceans, lakes and rivers. The natives of Goldenblue simply called themselves the People. They came in one variety, two genders, and quite a few political beliefs, all of them primitive by Matthews' standards (or, rather, within his experience, which was limited to more advanced, high-tech, starfaring societies).

As his wounds healed, he began wondering if there was anything salvageable from his ship, and one day he enticed a few locals into joining him as he tried to find it. It was a two-day march, and once there one look convinced him that there was absolutely nothing of use, nothing in anything remotely resembling working order, on or inside the wreck. His heart went out to the consciousness the ship had once possessed, and for the first time in his adult life he uttered a short prayer, hoping that it had found peace and perhaps even comfort in that limbo where self-aware machines went when they died.

On the way back, they heard a low growl off to their right, and a moment later a carnivore the size of a large lion broke cover and approached them. Matthews's three companions held their spears at the ready.

"That'll never stop him," said Matthews.

"We will do our best," replied one. "Keep going while we hold him at bay."

"I don't desert my friends," said Matthews, drawing his laser pistol and stepping forward.

"He will kill you."

"I don't think so," replied Matthews. He aimed at the dirt between the beast's feet and squeezed the firing mechanism. The creature roared and backed away a few feet.

"Magic!" breathed one of his companions.

"Science," replied Matthews. Then: "Stay alert! He's not going away."

The carnivore gathered itself as if about to charge, and Matthews fired again, this time burning the beast's left dew claw off. It screamed in pain and surprise, and this time retreated in earnest.

"Magic!" repeated his companion.

"Have it your way," said Matthews, who didn't relish spending the next hour explaining the scientific principles behind lasers.

"Can this thing actually kill the beast, Garmat?" asked another.

Matthews nodded his head. "Yes."

"Then why did you not?"

"Where I come from we don't eat carnivores," replied Matthews. "Do you?"

"No."

"Then why kill it when I can scare it away? It may have cubs. Why kill four or five creatures with one blast if I don't have to?"

"I shall have to think on that," was the reply.

"Good," said Matthews. "It'll give you something to do on the walk back."

16

It was three weeks later that a runner came through Bligori's village, warning them that "the rulers" were approaching.

"Who the hell are the rulers?" Matthews wanted to know.

"They live in the big village" – the language had no word for *city*– "some three days to the north of us," answered Bligori. "Once a year they come and take some of our food and some of our women."

"Do you approve of this?" asked Matthews.

"No, but if we defy them they will begin killing us until we do as we are told." Suddenly he grinned. "But now that we have you and your magic weapon…"

"There are limits to my magic," said Matthews, who knew that he would never be able to re-charge the pistol once he'd drained its power. "Let's see if reason works first."

"It never has. We kill one of them, they kill four or seven or nine of us."

Matthews smiled. "Let's try a different kind of reason."

"But if it doesn't work, you will kill them all, Garmat," said Bligori with certainty.

"What would you do with a thousand corpses rotting just outside the village?"

"Celebrate!" said Bligori happily.

"Let's see if we can celebrate an accommodation with them instead," said Matthews.

"I do not understand you, Garmat. If you can kill all your enemies, why not do so?"

"That's a lot of spears and knives," answered Matthews. "Why not turn them into friends and allies instead?"

"The creature you refused to kill when she threatened you a few weeks ago, when you first used your magic weapon," began Bligori. "Yes, I heard about it. Did you turn *her* into an ally?"

"No," replied Matthews. "But maybe, if she has young and they go hunting with her, and she refuses to attack some of the People because she remembers her experience, perhaps it will train or convince *them* not to attack the People either."

"I think you expect too much of our flesh eaters and our enemies."

"Perhaps," acknowledged Matthews. "But I always have the magic weapon if all else fails."

"Why give it a chance to fail?" asked Bligori in frustration.

You'd never understand notion of energy drain, and besides I think everyone's happier believing that it's magic.

"I just believe in giving everyone a chance to join us before punishing them for not doing do," said Matthews at last.

Bligori stared over Matthews' shoulder and pointed to a column of smoke.

"They will get their chance," he said. "Based on the smoke, I would say they are two days away."

17

Bligori was only wrong by a couple of hours.

The army marched into the village just two days and one hour later. The leader demanded that everyone gather in front of his warriors and explained that he had come for food and females, as usual.

"I think it is time for you to grow your own food and bed your own females," replied Bligori, stepping forward and staring at him with no show of concern.

"You are Bligori, are you not?" demanded the leader.

"You know that I am."

"What has gotten into you?" persisted the leader. "I will forgive you this one time, but I will tolerate no more insubordination."

"And we will tolerate no more abuse," replied Bligori.

Goddamn it, thought Matthews. *Didn't you hear a word I said?*

"I order you one more time," said the leader. "Turn over forty bundles of food and ten females."

Bligori folded his arms across his chest and stared at the leader.

"You have been warned!" snapped the leader. He turned to the three nearest warriors and made a quick gesture with his hands. All three stepped forward, spears at the ready.

Suddenly there was a humming sound, a brief flash of light, and all three warriors fell to the ground, screaming in pain, their feet blackened by the burn of a laser pistol.

"Go home," said Matthew, walked forward until he stood beside Bligori.

"Who are you?" demanded the leader. "In fact, *what* are you?"

"I am a member of the village."

"You?" scoffed the leader. "You are not even one of the People."

"I am now," said Matthews. He pointed the laser pistol at the leader. "And now I think you and your thugs had better leave."

"Kill them now!" demanded Bligori.

"Kill!" shouted most of the members of the village.

"I can, you know," said Matthews to the leader. "Do you want me to prove it, or will you leave?"

The leader glared at him, but didn't move.

"He will not obey you, Garmat," said Bligori. "He must die."

"He is considering his options," replied Matthews. "When he realizes that he has only two – to leave or to die – he'll make the proper choice."

After another full minute had passed the leader turned to his warriors and ordered them to follow him as he left the village.

"I will not forget this – or you!" were his parting words.

"Good," said Matthews. "I'd hate to have to do this all over again."

And then they were gone.

"Post a lookout to make sure they don't come back after dark," said Matthews. "They are not a happy crew."

"You should have killed them all with your magic flame," said Bligori unhappily.

"They'd just come back in greater numbers next year," answered Matthews.

"Then you would do it again."

"There is a limit to my magic," said Matthews. "And even if I killed them all this year and against next year, they would be back again and again, and even if they are slow learners, they would know by the third or fourth year to attack the village from afar, to hurl flaming spears into it, to kill all your meat animals and destroy your fields, to do all the damage they could do without ever entering the village." He paused. "And it would make no difference whether they killed you with their spears or burned and starved you from afar. Either way you'd be just as dead."

"But they will come back anyway," protested Bligori. "At least this way you could have shown them how deadly it is to attack *our* village, and they would have concentrated on all the other villages, villages that don't have a magic weapon."

"Why are they powerful?" replied Matthews, and then answered his own question. "They are powerful because their warriors are well fed, because they keep producing healthy new generations of warriors, because they have convinced you to give them whatever they ask for."

"But we will not do so any longer, because of your magic weapon."

Matthews looked around to make sure no one else could overhear them. "I'm going to let you in on a secret he said, one you must share with no one else. Do you agree?"

Bligori nodded his head.

"All right," continued Matthews. "My magic weapon is very old. In fact, it is dying. It can produce a flame perhaps thirty more times, perhaps less, and then it will be dead."

"Truly?"

"Truly."

"Then we have lost," said Bligori.

"Not necessarily," said Matthews. "I want your best craftsmen to make ten, twenty, one hundred copies of the magic weapon."

"We can make copies that are the same shape, and the same size, but they will not shine like yours, and they will not hum while spitting out a thin flame."

"Don't worry about that. They will never be asked to."

"Then I do not understand."

"When the warriors return next year, they will make the same demands as today, and I will burn their feet, or perhaps their arms, just as I did today. And I will make sure my weapon is covered with dust and dirt so that it does not shine. Then, with our best trackers to help me, I will follow them to every village they go to, and do the same thing." Matthews smiled. "And when we leave each village, we will leave behind a copy of the magic weapon. When the warriors come back, the chief of the village, or some warrior he chooses, will produce the weapon and threaten to burn them all to ashes if they do not leave and promise never to return."

"It is a lie."

"Let me give you a new word," said Matthews with a smile. "It is a *bluff.*"

18

And it worked. For three years the *faux* laser pistols held the army at bay.

Then the inevitable happened. A warrior, either feeling very full of himself or perhaps very full of something he drank, did not back down when challenged with a mock pistol, no flame shot forth, and as a punishment for deceiving the army the village was burned to the ground and all of its male members were killed.

This happened to three more villages in the next week when word reached Matthews of what was happening.

"Shit!" he said. "I'm going to have to go burn a few of them to convince them that at least *some* of the pistols are real."

He went out on his own – he knew the landscape well enough by then not to need a tracker – and confronted the army twice within the following week, inflicting some severe but non-fatal burns on the warriors.

Another village was destroyed a few days later, and this time he made sure he was confronting the very warriors who were responsible for it, and killed four of them, warning the rest never to show their faces around any of the villages again.

This went on for another fifty days. He knew he was on borrowed time, that eventually one of the enemy would figure out that the only time anyone ever got burned was when Matthews was wielding the weapon, but he didn't know what else to do, how else to protect what he now thought of as his own people.

It was as he was returning home after holding off the army in a distant village that they followed his trail (which he had made no attempt to hide), fell on him when he was asleep, and carted him off to the city, a primitive municipality that held some fifty thousand inhabitants living in the equivalent of shanties, but a place of sprawling luxury compared to the villages.

They tied him up in a small structure, and the next morning the commander of the army came up to him, laser pistol in hand, pointed it at his head, and squeezed the firing mechanism…and except for a feeble buzzing sound that soon ended, nothing happened.

What a perfect time to run out of power, thought Matthews. *I couldn't have timed it any better if I'd tried.*

The commander left, and as the day wore on Matthews became aware of the sounds of hammering, and based on his experiences on Kaus and Greenbriar and the others, he was pretty sure he knew what was happening.

In late afternoon they carried him outside, where the cross was waiting for him. They lifted him up to it, nailed his hands and feet onto it, and then attached a small sign behind his head.

It can't say INRI, he thought. *There's never been a Jew on this planet.* He turned his head to read the four alien letters, but his vision was blurred by pain and he couldn't make them out. *I hate to die without knowing what or who I'm the king of…*

He tried unsuccessfully to ignore the agony in his hands and feet. *Could be worse. Physical pain has got to be easier to bear than the emotional anguish the poor ship suffered.*

He felt a gentle hand on his left ankle and looked down. It was Bligori.

"You will not be forgotten," he whispered. "Already we are preparing ourselves for the battle to come, and our battle cry will be 'Garmat!'"

Ah, hell – I didn't want to be a Prince of Peace anyway.

"We will resist, and we will kill, and we will not rest until those of the cities treat those of the villages as they themselves wish to be treated. Whatever hardships we must undergo, whatever battles we must wage, however long it takes, the Order of the Magic Flame shall endure and triumph."

Matthews felt his consciousness slipping away as Bligcri promised blood and battle without end, but he had one last sentence to utter, not for his captors but those who had become his followers.

"Forgive them, Father," he whispered just before he expired, "for they know exactly what they do."

❧The End❧

Made in the USA
Las Vegas, NV
20 September 2022

55653437R00104